D1091587

SLEEP TILL NOON

books by MAX SHULMAN

BAREFOOT BOY WITH CHEEK

THE FEATHER MERCHANTS

THE ZEBRA DERBY

SLEEP TILL NOON

sleep till noon

MAX SHULMAN

ILLUSTRATED BY BILL CRAWFORD

DOUBLEDAY & COMPANY, INC.

Garden City, New York, 1953

The characters, the location, and the incidents in this book are
entirely the product of the author's imagination and
have no relation to any person or event in real life.

Printed in the United States
at the Country Life Press, Garden City, N. Y.

AMENDED DEDICATION

The first edition of this book was dedicated to Dan, Bud, Pete, and Nick. This requires a word of explanation.

At the time the first edition went to press my wife and I had three sons—Dan, Bud, and Pete. We were expecting a fourth child who, we assumed, of course, would be a boy, and for whom we had chosen the name Nick. Hence the dedication.

As it turned out, however, the fourth child was a girl. "Well," I said to my wife, "we will have to call her Nick."

"We will not," replied my wife with a rush of feeling.

So we called her Martha, and this edition is dedicated to Dan, Bud, Pete, and Martha.

Sorry, Nick.

One chapter of this material appeared in altered form in *Cosmopolitan* magazine.

SLEEP TILL NOON

CHAPTER 1

Bang! Bang! Bang! Bang!

Four shots ripped into my groin, and I was off on the biggest adventure of my life . . .

But first let me tell you a little about myself. My name is Harry Riddle, and I am a sensitive, retiring person. Even as a boy this was true. I remember numerous times when the neighborhood children would say to me, "Come on, Harry. We're going out and hold up a filling station," and I would answer, not unkindly, "No, thanks, fellows. I'm going to stay home and read."

I suppose I missed a great deal by not participating in these normal activities of childhood. Certainly I should have been better prepared for the hurly-burly of later life. But somehow I could not find it in myself to join my young colleagues in their robust games. Occasionally I would try. Once, I recall, I let myself be persuaded to accompany my friends on a purse-snatching expedition. I seized the handbag of an elderly lady, but she tripped me with her crutch and held me by the collar until the police came—a matter of forty minutes.

On that occasion, I remember, my mother knocked me insensible. My father said nothing, but I could tell he was displeased.

My father and I are a great deal alike, he, too, being a sensitive, retiring person. He, in fact, retired in 1924, a victim of technological unemployment. Dad, as I like to call him, is a capmaker by profession. When men unaccountably stopped wearing caps after the Coolidge election, he was thrown out of work and has not worked since. He has not, however, lost hope that this current hat fad will pass.

Dad and I are, as I said, a great deal alike, but Mother (my mother) is a horse of a different color, she should excuse the expression. She is a hale, extroverted woman, given to bursts of temper. Many is the time Dad and I have fled, laughing, from the house with great, running welts on the backs of our heads.

Mother always carried a darning egg in the toe of a long black stocking, and she would hit us with it when she grew angry. A short while ago, when I was visiting her, I twitted her good-naturedly about the darning egg, and she hit me with it again. They had to take stitches.

It must not be supposed that my home was a scene of continual violence. No indeed. At night, when Mother went downtown to scrub floors, Dad and I would sit and

Dad

have long, tranquil discussions. Even as a boy my thoughts were of a cosmic nature. Whither are we drifting? I would wonder. What is the world coming to? Is there hope for mankind? What can I best do to fulfill my destiny as an American and a human being? All these questions would tumble from my lips as Dad listened patiently, rocking back and forth in his chair. (The chair, incidentally, was not a rocker; its two front legs were missing.) "What is the answer?" I would demand. "What must I do?"

"You must do like I tell ya," he would reply. His speech was rough; he had had no education except in what I like to call the School of Hard Knocks. "Get rich, boy," he would say, filling his corncob pipe with cigarette butts I had collected for him during the day. "Get rich, boy. Then sleep till noon and screw 'em all."

I have often thought of having a small volume of Dad's aphorisms printed. When good vellum is available again, perhaps I shall.

Far into the night Dad would speak to me, and I would listen intently, grasping, in spite of my tender years, the full import of his wise advice. When Dad told me to get rich, he meant that I should accumulate large sums of money. Boy though I was, I understood that.

We would talk and talk until Dad dozed off and toppled from his chair. I would carry him to his pallet and tuck him in. Then I would retire to my own pallet and think about getting rich until my little eyelids grew heavy and closed in sleep. Sometimes I would read a book on how to increase your income. *Up Your Bracket,* it was called.

And in the mornings there was school. School! Here I came into my own. Positions were reversed; I was the leader, not the laggard, among the other children. In neighborhood games like Squish (dropping safes on policemen) they were admittedly better than I, but in school it was different. I read better, drew better, sang better. I knew all the answers to all the questions. I got the highest marks. All this was a great satisfaction to me, and not one whit lessened by the fact that the other children took off my trousers and threw them on top of a passing bus every day after school.

Almost as much as I am beholden to my father for guidance, I am in the debt of Miss Spinnaker, my sixth-grade teacher, whom I credit with instilling in me my great thirst for learning. Let me hasten to state that all my other teachers were also fine, upstanding women, and they taught me a good deal in their classes. But they were inclined to be abrupt with me when I dropped in at their homes in the evening to discuss the day's lessons.

Not so Miss Spinnaker. She welcomed me with great enthusiasm whenever I called. On each visit we would take up a different topic: names of state capitals, deciduous trees, game fish of North America, the decimal system, the lyric poems of Longfellow, and similar subjects. She would ask me questions, holding me on her lap and fondling me with innocent abandon as I recited. In accordance with her wishes, I fondled her too. Afterward, hot and tired, we would have tall glasses of ginger beer.

My mother broke in on us one night and hit us both with

Mother

her darning egg. I never went to Miss Spinnaker's home again, although we remained the best of friends and fondled one another amicably when we met in the corridor at school.

I was graduated high in my class at grammar school, and I finished with equal distinction at high school. Then I went out to look for a job. At this time I was eighteen years old, slender, fair, and, in all modesty, not unattractive. My clothes were patched but clean, and my appearance was of a type to inspire confidence in a prospective employer. You may be sure that I soon found a responsible position: bus boy in an all-night cafeteria.

The years I worked in the cafeteria, I can honestly say, are among the most cherished of my life. Although my pay was niggardly, I was immeasurably enriched by the contacts I made. It was at the cafeteria that I met two men who deserve places alongside my father and Miss Spinnaker as people who shaped my life. One was Walter Obispo; the other was George Overmeyer.

Obispo was a silver-haired man of sixty, an attorney who had been disbarred for some trifling offense. He used to sit in the cafeteria all night, explaining that he preferred it to the huge town house where he lived alone. I understood, for I, too, have been lonely. Who has not? Eh? Who has not?

As often as I could take time off from my various duties, which included clearing tables, washing dishes, mopping floors, emptying garbage, ejecting drunks, and adding benzoate of soda to the tainted meat which made it possible for us to sell our meals so reasonably, I would bring a fresh cup of coffee to Obispo and we would talk. I would listen breathlessly as he told me of his experiences as a lawyer—how he had bribed jurors, suborned perjury, stolen state

Walter Obispo

exhibits, and leaped on the backs of ambulances going as rapidly as sixty miles an hour. He never tired of telling his stories, nor I of listening to them.

George Overmeyer was much younger than Obispo. He was, I would say, in his late twenties—a thin man with pinched features and intense, blazing eyes. He, too, used to spend his nights in the cafeteria, but not in conversation.

He would bring in heavy tomes on sociology and economics and history and sit reading and making notes. Often he would just sit and think—or, rather, worry. An expression of such great concern would come over his face that the heart within me would ache. One night, when he looked particularly distressed, I made bold to speak.

"Excuse me, friend," I said. "Would you care to tell me what worries you?"

"Oh, nothing much," he replied. "The world, mankind, civilization, social justice, democracy, human rights . . ."

I nodded understandingly, for I, too, used to worry about these very topics until Dad had provided me with the answer. "I can help you," I said.

"Oh, peachy," said George.

"The thing to do," I said, "is to get rich. Then sleep till noon and screw 'em all."

He leaped up. "Good God, man, that's it!" he cried. He wrung my hand gratefully. "How can I ever thank you?"

"The knowledge that I have helped you is thanks enough," I said simply, and we shook hands again, silently this time, not trusting ourselves to speak.

"Get rich," he mused. "Now why couldn't I think of that?"

"Sometimes," I said, "one gets so involved in a problem that one can't see the trees for the forest."

"What a striking phrase!" he exclaimed. "Mind if I jot it down?"

I waved my hand graciously and he made the entry in his notebook.

"I take it that you are rich," he said. "Just working here for a lark."

"Well, no," I confessed, "but it's only a matter of time."

"Perhaps you'll have me over for tea sometime when you get your mansion."

"Happy to," I said cordially. "I'm not the kind of person who's going to forget poor wretches like you just because I'm rich."

"Commendable," he murmured.

"No, sir," I said. "I'm going to do good works when I get rich. I've already got a few charities in mind—free Muzak for nursing mothers, relief tubes for indigent aviators, and lots of other greathearted plans."

"This makes me very happy," said George. "I'm so glad to hear that money will leave you as sweet and imbecilic as you are today. Money, you know, sometimes has a tendency to corrupt."

"It does?" I said with some alarm. This, indeed, was an aspect that had not occurred to me. I wanted to be rich, yes, but not if it meant being corrupted. There is no price high enough, I always say, to pay for a man's integrity.

"Yes, there *have* been scattered cases of people being corrupted by money," he said. "But don't worry about it."

But I *did* worry about it. In fact, I could not get it out of my mind. Was it, I kept thinking, worth the risk? Was getting rich worth taking the chance of becoming corrupted, of losing my sterling honesty, my profound humaneness, the saintliness that made me such a rare man among men? The question stayed with me waking and sleeping.

One night while I was grinding hamburger in the kitchen of the cafeteria and thinking about my problem, I inadvertently stuck my hand into the grinder. I must have cried out, because in an instant the kitchen was filled with people, among them the proprietor who gave me a waiver of damages to sign with my good hand. At this moment Obispo leaped forward with a full-throated cry, wrenched the waiver from me, and announced that he was representing me. I had time to give him a grateful smile before I fainted.

A few days later Obispo came to the hospital and gave me one thousand dollars, which he said was my share of the five-thousand-dollar settlement he had received for my accident. For a moment I could not speak. One thousand dollars and all mine! It was overwhelming. I blinked back my tears and smiled wanly at my benefactor.

Then suddenly an idea sprang full-blown into my brain. Here was the answer to my great problem. All at once I knew how to get rich and yet stay uncorrupted: I would become a lawyer.

It was so obvious. Lawyers helped people. For helping people they got large sums of money. Consider Obispo: he had done me an immense kindness in getting a thousand dollars for me. At the same time he had earned four thousand dollars for himself. So, in a single operation, he had performed an act both lucrative and eleemosynary.

And I, as a lawyer, would do the same. Become rich by earning large fees. Remain uncorrupted by doing good deeds for people. And do both at the same time, that was the beauty part.

I hastened to tell Obispo of my decision to become a lawyer. I said I would use my thousand dollars to go to college and read the law. But he had a much better idea. There was no need for me to go off to college, study for six years, and then perhaps fail to pass the bar. I could give him the thousand dollars and read the law in his office. It would take only a few months, and he would guarantee that I passed the bar. My throat was too filled with tears to speak; I could only nod in grateful agreement.

So upon my discharge from the hospital I started to report every day to Obispo's office in the back of the High Life Billiard Parlor to read his law library. This did not take very long, since his library consisted of only one book —*City Ordinances of Winnipeg.* Within six months I became possibly the world's foremost authority on the municipal statutes of Winnipeg and also a middling expert at Kelly pool, which I played with my tutor during his informal lectures. Obispo believed strongly that relaxation was the key to learning. He considered playing pool during lectures an excellent means of relieving tension. Nor were his lectures crammed with abstruse and difficult legal data. Usually, in fact, they were not about the law at all, but about women. He was quite inventive in the love-making line, and in later years I spent many pleasurable hours approximating those of the conformations he had described to me that were not beyond my agility.

Beguiling though my days were with Obispo, I sometimes was troubled about the casual way my education was proceeding. "Do you really think I'll be ready for the bar examination?" I asked him frequently, and he always replied, "Don't worry about a thing."

He was right. When the time came to take my bar examination, I passed with flying colors—that is to say, Mr. Weatherwax did. (I should explain that Mr. Weatherwax was the man Obispo hired to take my bar examination for me.)

I could hardly wait to rush home and show Mother and Dad my law diploma. "Mother! Dad!" I cried as I burst into our squalid quarters. "Come see my diploma. I'm a lawyer. No more working in a cafeteria for me!"

"Don't give me that crap," said Mother. "You quit that job and I'll knock you through the wall."

Dad sprang to my defense. "You leave him be," he said. "Harry's gonna be a big man someday, like I'da been if I had his education."

"The only way you'd be a big man," said Mother, "is if somebody blew you up."

"Darning eggs and stones will break my bones," said Dad, "but names will never hurt me."

This was a brave little lie on Dad's part, for he was the most sensitive of men, and Mother's thoughtless allusions to his lack of initiative injured him far more than her frequent blows. Mother did not really mean to be unkind. Underneath her bluster I knew there was a genuine affection for Dad. I must admit, though, that she concealed it perfectly.

The argument raged on. Mother flailed me with her darning egg until my head looked like a Hubbard squash, but I was adamant. The following week I put a down payment on some office furniture, rented an abandoned streetcar, and hung out my shingle. I got the shingle free from a friend of mine who worked at a roofing company, and I lettered it myself.

HARRY RIDDLE

ATTORNEY AT LAW

Specializing in City Ordinances of Winnipeg

proclaimed the shingle.

I was in business.

CHAPTER 2

It would be idle to pretend that I was a successful lawyer from the start. The first case I pleaded, in fact, turned out very badly. Although I conducted the defense with much zeal, my client was given five years at hard labor. This sentence reflects little credit on me when you consider that he had only been charged with overtime parking.

Honesty compels me to admit that I fared no better in my second case. I was representing a man whose unscrupulous relatives wished him adjudged insane so they could get control of his fortune. After the third day of the hearing the judge ruled against my client, remarking dryly that only a lunatic would have retained me as counsel.

For a long time after that I had no cases. I tried for a while to earn my living as an income-tax consultant, but only one client came to me, and he took his business elsewhere when he learned that I had computed his taxes to be 30 per cent more than his gross income.

It is always darkest before the dawn, I like to say. Certainly circumstances could have been no more unpromising than they were at the moment I received the assignment that led to my present exalted position. I had been evicted from my streetcar for non-payment of rent. My furniture had been repossessed. Also my suit. I had a concussion from my mother's darning egg. In the midst of all this blackness, like a ray of light, a message arrived: Judge Ralph Schram wanted to see me.

I was in his chambers at the appointed hour, my hair neatly brushed, my clothes patched but clean, a deferential smile on my lips.

"Wipe that stupid smirk off your face," said the judge in greeting.

I was not deceived by his gruffness. I felt sure that he was basically a kindly man and that the story about his spending every Sunday at the state prison gloating over the inmates he had committed was apocryphal.

"Listen carefully," he continued, "because I haven't got much time. It's Saturday afternoon and I've got to catch a train up to the state prison so I can spend Sunday gloating over the inmates I have committed."

"Yes, your honor," I said briskly.

"I have to appoint a public defender in a trial that is coming up next Monday. The defendant is so palpably guilty that no lawyer with an ounce of brains will touch the case. So I called you."

"I hope you will find me worthy of your confidence," I said simply.

"His name is Sam Hiff and he's in the county jail," said the judge and threw me out of the room, indicating that the interview was over.

Judge Ralph Schram

I went at once to see Sam Hiff, whom I found to be an attractive cross-eyed man with eczema. "How do you do?" I said. "I'm Harry Riddle and I've been appointed by the court to represent you."

"They couldn't get nobody else, huh?" asked Hiff.

I shook my head.

"You look pretty stupid, hey."

I made a *moue.*

"Well," he shrugged, "I guess I'm stuck with you, hey."

"That's the spirit, Mr. Hiff," I said, clapping his fat back. "Now let's get down to business. If I'm to be your attorney, I will require you to be absolutely truthful with me. First of all, Mr. Hiff, are you innocent?"

"Yeh," he replied.

I seized his hand thankfully. "That's what I wanted to hear, Mr. Hiff. You may rest assured that I will leave no stone unturned in my efforts to disprove this monstrous accusation that has been brought against you. Trust me, Mr. Hiff, trust me."

Giving his hand a final squeeze, I left the cell. When I got home later, it occurred to me that I should have asked him what he was accused of. But I decided not to go back and ask him, thinking that such a move might impair his confidence in me.

The case of the State vs. Sam Hiff opened at nine o'clock Monday morning under the able direction of Judge Ralph Schram, who threatened to disbar both Swanson, the district attorney, and me if we did not wind up the trial in time for him to attend an execution early that afternoon. In the interests of speed, Swanson and I picked the jury by the simple process of accepting the first twelve veniremen who came before us, notwithstanding the fact that four of them were deaf-mutes. By nine-twenty the jury was sworn, and Swanson rose to deliver the opening statement of the prosecution.

At this moment I was still not aware of the charge against Sam Hiff, but I was not disturbed. I was sure that I would learn the charge from Swanson's opening address and that I could prepare an instant rebuttal. In addition to being a sensitive, retiring person, I am also a quick thinker.

"Ladies and gentlemen of the jury," said Swanson with a nervous glance at Judge Schram, who sat frowning over a stop watch, "I will not waste your time with any long oration. The state intends to bring this trial swiftly to its inevitable conclusion . . ."

"Come on, come on," snapped Judge Schram.

"We will prove," continued Swanson, "that the defendant Hiff has large deposits in several banks, that he has various sources of income, that he lives in a luxurious apartment filled with costly furniture. At the conclusion of the State's case, you will have no choice except to find the defendant guilty as charged. Thank you." He sat down.

I could only conclude from Swanson's remarks that Hiff was on trial for being a wealthy man. I did not know when the possession of large sums of money had been made a crime, for I had not kept up with recent legislation, but I was filled with a sense of outrage. This kind of thing struck at the very fundament of our republic. This was no longer merely the case of the State vs. Sam Hiff; this was Americanism vs. un-Americanism, totalitarianism vs. democracy. I leaped to my feet and strode across the court to the jury.

"I trust counsel for the defense will not dawdle for forty-three seconds as did the prosecution," said Judge Schram.

"Ladies and gentlemen of the jury," I said rapidly, "what I have to say is brief. Sam Hiff is a rich man. I say this proudly. Sam Hiff is a rich man . . ."

There was a puzzled murmur among the spectators, and Judge Schram jailed them all for contempt.

"If you return a verdict of guilty against the wealthy defendant Hiff," I continued, "you will be returning a verdict of guilty against George Washington, Thomas Jefferson, Andrew Carnegie, Bernard Baruch, and other Americans who have made this country great. Thank you."

I sat down and noted with satisfaction the effects of my speech. The jurors sat stupefied, looking at each other askance. At the prosecution table Swanson and his assistants were in animated conversation. The reporters covering the trial were rushing to telephones. Even Judge Schram was impressed; he sat shaking his head slowly.

"Well," I said to Hiff with permissible pride, "what did you think of that?"

"I didn't know that Washington and Carnegie and Baruch and all them guys was relief chiselers, hey," he said.

"What?" I said.

"I didn't know they took relief checks from the county welfare board like I done."

"Mr. Hiff," I said, aghast, "can you possibly mean that you are charged with accepting relief checks while you had a private income?"

"How do you like that, hey?" mused Hiff. "George Washington! I never even knew they *had* relief in them days."

I could see it was true. "Mr. Hiff," I said frankly, "I have made a terrible mistake."

"Don't worry about it, hey," he answered, baring his Hutchinson's teeth in a kindly smile. "You just prove that Washington and them guys was relief chiselers and they ain't a jury in the country would convict me."

"Mr. Hiff," I said, "if you wish to retain another counsel, I stand ready to withdraw."

"You nuts?" he asked, giving me a playful push. "If I hire myself a mouthpiece, then they know I got dough and I'm licked. I got to take whatever they give me, even a punk like you, hey. But," he added, "I got to admit you sure pulled one out of the hat. George Washington! Jeez!"

"Mr. Hiff, there's something you must know. George Washington was not a relief chiseler, nor any of those people I mentioned."

His jaw flew open. "So why," he asked in a strangled voice, "did you tell the jury I was a rich man, hey?"

"It was an error," I admitted with a wry smile. "But not irreparable," I added. "In the first place, four of the jurors didn't hear me. As for the rest, I am confident that I can prove to them that you are a poor man and needed those relief checks. For, by your own admission, Mr. Hiff, you are innocent, and I offer you my solemn pledge that you will be freed."

"What," he cried, clutching his head with both hands, "did I get myself into? Why didn't I cop a plea?"

"Truth crushed to earth," I continued, "shall rise again. Depend on me, Mr. Hiff. I shall not fail you."

"Ah, shaddup," said the defendant.

"The State will damn well call its first witness," said Judge Schram.

Swanson promptly called a man named Homer Lascoulie, who was rushed to the witness chair by two bailiffs and hurriedly sworn. "What is your occupation, Mr. Lascoulie?" asked Swanson.

"I am cashier of the First National Bank."

"Are you familiar with the defendant Hiff?"

"Yes, I have seen him at the bank making deposits on many occasions."

Swanson walked over to the exhibits table, picked up a large filing card, and returned to the witness. "Do you recognize this card, Mr. Lascoulie?"

"Yes. It is one of the cards we use at the bank to record the balances of depositors."

Swanson handed him the card. "Will you read the name on the card, please?"

"Sam Hiff."

"Now will you read the balance which is recorded there?"

"$14,896.20."

"The State offers this card in evidence as Exhibit A," said Swanson.

"I object, your worship," I cried, rising to my feet.

"Ah, shaddup," said Judge Schram.

"Your witness," said Swanson to me.

"No questions," I said, for indeed I could not think of any.

Swanson then called in rapid succession the cashier of the Farmers and Merchants National Bank, who testified that Hiff had $9,106.53 on deposit there, the cashier of the Main Street Savings Bank, who testified that Hiff had $4,653.08 on deposit there, the cashier of the Commercial Bank and Trust Company, who testified that Hiff had $17,094.80 on deposit there, a man named One-Eye Harrison, who testified that he was employed in a billiard parlor owned by Hiff, a man named Brains Ellingboe, who testified that he was employed in a pinball-machine business owned by Hiff, a man named Dirtyface Hogan, who testified that he was employed in a bar and grill owned by Hiff, the landlord of the Elmhurst Park Towers, who testified that Hiff paid $400 a month for his quarters in that apartment house, the manager of the Bon-Ton Furniture Emporium, who testified that Hiff had paid him $8,965.38 to furnish his apartment, and the manager of the Bicycle Playing Cards Corporation, who testified that Hiff had ordered a boxcar of pinochle decks from him.

Although I was sure that there was some simple explanation to account for all the facts brought out by these witnesses, I could not for the moment think of it and I was forced to let them all go without cross-examination. I kept patting Hiff's arm reassuringly through all the testimony, but he did not seem to take much comfort from it. He sat

Esme Geddes

slack-jawed and dull-eyed—until the State called Esme Geddes to the stand. Then he perked up.

"Lookit, hey," he said eagerly to me as Miss Geddes took the witness chair. "Now there is my idea of a real piece."

It was mine too, frankly, but I should not have put it so

vulgarly. Miss Geddes did not have the spare frame that is so highly regarded by modern young women; she had instead a toothsome sleekness. There was flesh on this girl, and although it did not sag, there was no place on her body that would not provide satisfaction to a man bent on pinching. Her face was round and pert, with full, soft lips and eyes of deep blue. Her hair was the color of honey.

A young woman of Miss Geddes's contours would ordinarily give the impression of voluptuousness, even carnality. Not so Miss Geddes. There was a levelness in her blue eyes, an attitude in her erect carriage that spoke only of good breeding, of honesty, straightforwardness, principle, and dignity. A fine young woman, it was clear. A noble young woman; an American princess.

"Did you ever see a pair of knockers like that in your life?" asked Hiff.

As a matter of fact, I had not, but I did not reply.

Miss Geddes settled herself in the witness chair and pulled her simple but expensive frock over her knees. She took the oath, Judge Schram pinched her, and Swanson began the questioning.

"Your name is Esme Geddes?"

"Yes."

"And you are with the county welfare board?"

"Yes."

"What kind of work do you do for the county welfare board?"

"Investigating relief clients, mainly. Sometimes I am

sent out to shame an unwed mother, but mainly I investigate relief clients."

"You were the investigator in the case of the defendant Hiff?"

"Yes. We became suspicious after he had called for his relief check several times in a chauffeur-driven car."

"Did you go to the defendant Hiff's apartment at the Elmhurst Park Towers?"

"Yes."

"Will you describe the apartment for his honor and the jury?"

"I cannot recommend its décor, but I am sure it was very expensively furnished. The marble bathtub in the living room alone must have cost ten thousand dollars."

"How did the defendant Hiff greet you when you arrived?"

"He kissed my hand."

"Romance 'em, I always say," said Hiff, tugging my arm. "A broad likes to be romanced, I don't care who it is."

I jerked my sleeve distastefully from his grasp.

"Then what happened, Miss Geddes?"

"He chased me around the marble bathtub until he became winded."

"I got to quit smoking," said Hiff to me.

I looked at him with loathing.

"Then what happened, Miss Geddes?"

"I asked him why he was on relief."

"What did he say?"

"He said he was out of work."

"What did you say?"

"I asked him what kind of work he did."

"What did he say?"

"He said he was a horsecar conductor."

"What did you say?"

"I asked him if he had tried to find another job."

"What did he say?"

"He said: 'What do you want to be a nosy Parker for? Sit down and I'll fix you a drink. You'll feel like a new broad.' "

"What did you say?"

"I declined with thanks."

"What did he say?"

"He pushed me down on a twenty-four-foot divan covered in cloth of gold and started to make advances."

"Yup," nodded Hiff. "That's what I did, hey."

I growled in my throat; there was a red film over my eyes.

"What did you say?"

"I said: 'Whatever can you be thinking of, Mr. Hiff?' "

"What did he say?"

"He did not answer the question but grasped me about the neck and proceeded to conduct himself in a most ungentlemanly manner."

That was too much. Seizing a volume of *Corpus Juris* which was lying on the defense table, I swung it with all my force into the mouth of the defendant Hiff. "You cad!" I shrieked. "You unspeakable, unspeakable cad!" I threw him to the floor and leaped up and down on his head. He scrambled to his feet and tried to run from the room, but I threw a small juror at him and knocked him down again. I should have certainly killed him had I not been overcome by several bailiffs.

At length I was quieted and placed in a restraining jacket to await contempt proceedings.

CHAPTER 3

I was so exhausted after my amok that I slept around the clock. Although sleeping in this circular position was uncomfortable, I managed to put in almost eight hours. Shortly after I woke, the jailer unlocked my cell and told me that my bail had been posted and I was free to go.

"Who paid my bail?" I asked the desk sergeant on my way out.

"I did," said a feminine voice.

"Why, Miss Geddes!" I exclaimed, for it was she.

My heart began to pound wildly at the sight of her, and I felt like leaping about the room fawn-fashion. But after my recent outburst, I thought I had better control my feelings, lest she think me unstable. I confined my enthusiasm to jumping up and down in a standing position.

"I hope you don't think I'm interfering," said Miss

Geddes. "I felt that the least I could do was to put up your bail after what you did for me."

"It was nothing that any red-blooded manic-depressive wouldn't have done," I murmured.

"You are too modest, Mr. Riddle," she said. "It was the most gallant act I have ever seen in my life."

I jumped up and down faster.

"Please," said the desk sergeant, "would you mind jumping someplace else? You're making the water in my foot bath slop over."

"Of course," I said. "Miss Geddes, would you like to go out for a good five-cent cup of coffee?"

"I'd love to," she replied, "but it must be Dutch treat."

"Very well," I smiled. I offered her my patched but clean arm and we went to a funny little place that I knew.

After we had finished laughing at the funny little place, we started to talk. "Tell me about yourself," I said.

"There's nothing much to tell," she disclaimed modestly. "I'm just like any other beautiful girl with superior breeding and intelligence."

"How do you happen to be working for the county welfare board?"

"It's only temporary. I'm gathering material for a paper about slums that I'm going to read to the Junior League."

"That must be fascinating," I said, clapping my hands. "Tell me about it."

"Well, I'm doing a survey of this city, showing the correlation between slum areas and crime. Here, I'll show you." She took a map of the city from her handbag and spread it on the table. "Here," she said, indicating an exclusive residential section on the edge of town, "there is very little crime. Here"—she pointed out a rather shabby residential section closer to the commercial district—"there is a marked increase in the crime rate. And here"—she laid her finger on a slum bordering the railroad tracks—"is a veritable nest of crime."

"That's where I live," I said.

"You do?" she asked, registering keen interest. "Are you a slum child?"

"I was," I smiled. "Now I guess you'd call me a slum man."

"But this is wonderful!" she exclaimed. "I've been wanting to get a good, intimate interview with a slum dweller. So far I've had no luck. I've tried to draw out some of the relief clients I've investigated, but they've all been so surly . . . downright hostile, some of them. One woman hit me with a darning egg."

"My mother, I'll wager," I chuckled.

"Do you mean that *you* live in that tar-paper hovel by the coalyards?"

I nodded modestly.

"This is better than I expected!" she cried happily. She took a notebook and pencil from her bag and put on a pair of tortoise-shell spectacles. "I'm so lucky that I found you."

"My feelings exactly," I said and reddened at my boldness.

"Would you mind answering a few questions, Mr. Riddle?"

"Anything. Anything at all."

She poised the pencil over the notebook. "Do you have pellagra?"

"No, ma'am."

"Hm," she said with some disappointment, but quickly rallied her spirits. "Do you find each crime easier to commit as you go along?"

"Well, I don't know——" I temporized.

"I had hoped, Mr. Riddle," she said coldly, "that *you* would be more co-operative."

"I'm sorry," I said. "Why, yes, I believe each crime would be successively easier."

She made an entry in the notebook. "Do you have sex fantasies in which your partner is a woman of superior economic means?"

"I'm having one now," I admitted with a blush.

She nodded and made another note. "How old were you when you began using narcotics?"

"Eighteen months," I said, remembering that paregoric is an opium derivative.

"Splendid!" she cried, her pencil flying. "You'd be a classic case if you only had pellagra."

"I'm sorry about the pellagra, Miss Geddes. If I had known, be assured that I would have contracted a case somewhere."

"You're sweet," she said and patted my hand.

"It would be difficult to be otherwise to you, dear lady," I replied with lowered eyelids.

"You know, Mr. Riddle, you seem to have more of the social graces than the other churls in your class."

"It is you who brings me out of myself."

"It might be amusing," she said speculatively, "to exhibit you to some of my friends."

"I'm a million laughs," I assured her.

"Maybe it's not such a good idea," she said, stroking her chin thoughtfully. "The last time I brought home a derelict to entertain my guests, he stole my brother."

"You may depend on me to behave in an exemplary manner," I said quietly.

She thought for a moment. "All right, I'll do it. Can you make it Saturday night?"

"It would be better sooner," I said. "By Saturday, Judge Schram will probably have me in jail for contempt."

"Oh, don't worry about that. I'll have my father get the charges dismissed."

"Well, if it isn't too much trouble——"

"Not at all. Daddy loves to bribe judges. Saturday night, then, Mr. Riddle."

"It will be my pleasure."

"Now I must go home," said Miss Geddes. "Can I drop you somewhere?"

"If it's not out of your way, I'm going home too."

"Come along," she said. We each laid down a nickel for the coffee and went outside to her cream-colored phaeton. I could not help but admire the authority with which she drove; we did not stop for a single traffic light all the way to my house, although they were all red.

She diminished her speed and I leaped from the car.

"Don't stop," I said as we approached my house, "or the children will steal your tires. Just slow down to thirty or so and I'll hop out."

"Righto," she said. "See you Saturday. Be sure to wear those funny clothes you've got on."

She diminished her speed and I leaped from the car. Laughing lightly at the resultant fractures, I went into the house with singing heart.

CHAPTER 4

Mother was reading in the living room when I came into the house. "Mother! Halloa! I have news!" I cried.

Mother looked up from the *Racing Form.* "Yeah?" she said.

"I'm in love," I declared.

"With a girl?"

I nodded.

"Thank God," said Mother.

CHAPTER 5

Several years ago in my town there lived a boy named Arthur Scott. His family was very poor, and young Scott was forced to go to work at an early age. Dressed in rags, he sold rag-paper editions of the evening papers on a street corner downtown. Each night, after he had sold all his papers, Scott would go home cold and hungry and turn over his meager earnings to his mother—except, of course, in summer, when he went home *hot* and hungry.

On his way home every night Scott passed one of the town's finest bakeries. The bakery window was filled with all manner of goodies, and the poor urchin would always stop and press his nose against the glass, salivating wildly at the sight of the cakes, pies, and *petit fours.* One night, filled with unusually acute longing, Scott pressed his nose too hard against the window. The window broke, and

Scott's nose was severely gashed. An ambulance was summoned and Scott was rushed to Mercy Hospital.

Although Mercy Hospital was a charitable institution, run by the city to provide free medical care to the indigent, some of the best doctors in the city practiced there—successful physicians who took time off from their lucrative private practices to devote as much as two or three hours a month to needy patients. Among these unselfish healers was the eminent plastic surgeon, Dr. Nelson Estabrook.

Dr. Estabrook was a man of wide interests. In addition to being a plastic surgeon, he was also a stock-market plunger. Daily he won or lost great sums of money on the stock exchange. He was in almost constant communication with his brokers. Even while he was operating, he kept a telephone beside him so that he could be instantly informed of any fluctuations in the market.

Dr. Estabrook happened to be on duty when young Scott was brought into the hospital to have his nose mended. Scott was immediately prepared for surgery and wheeled into the operating room where Dr. Estabrook stood in readiness. After a brief examination, Dr. Estabrook went swiftly to work.

"Scalpel," he said, and the nurse handed him a scalpel.

"Trephine," he said, and the nurse handed him a trephine.

"Clamp," he said, and the nurse handed him a clamp.

"Telephone," he said, and the nurse handed him a telephone.

He dialed a number. "Hello," he said. "Let me talk to Merrill Lynch, Pierce, Fenner, or Beane. . . . Hello, Fenner. What's happening to North American Locomotive? . . . Still going down? . . . You need another half million? . . . But I've already given you two million today. . . . All right. Sell my house, car, yacht, and racing stables. . . . Let me know as soon as anything happens. Good-by."

Dr. Estabrook returned to the operation with a heavy heart. North American Locomotive had fallen two hundred points that day. An unscrupulous competitor had started a rumor that a drop-forge operator at the North American Locomotive Works had leprosy, and railroads all over the country were canceling orders. Dr. Estabrook had his entire fortune invested in North American Locomotive; a further drop in the stock would wipe him out.

Preoccupied with locomotives, Dr. Estabrook scarcely noticed what he was doing with young Scott's nose. Absently he dismantled the nose and proceeded to reassemble it. The nurse watched him silently for a while, but finally curiosity forced her to speak. "Doctor," she said, "how come you made his nose look like a cowcatcher?"

"Oh, pshaw," said the doctor, irritated at himself. "Now I've got to do it all over. Scalpel."

But before the nurse could hand him the scalpel, the phone rang. Dr. Estabrook seized it eagerly. "Yes?" he cried.

"North American just dropped ten more points," he was told

The doctor blanched, teetered for a moment, and then dropped dead.

"Oh, pshaw," said the nurse. "Now we will have to leave this boy's nose looking like a cowcatcher, for the late Dr. Estabrook was the only plastic surgeon we had."

Two weeks later young Scott was discharged from the hospital, in perfect health but sullen. The giggles he had provoked from the nurses at the hospital were nothing compared to the reception he got at home. He was greeted with guffaws and thigh-slapping from his family and friends. "Hey, lookit old Cowcatcher Nose," they cried and rolled over and over with laughter.

All this derision was psychologically devastating to Cowcatcher Nose, as young Scott was now called. His former sweet nature curdled. He became surly and abrupt. Where he had previously been gregarious, he now avoided people. His industry was replaced by sloth. His mouth, in the past much given to smiling, now curved unpleasantly downward under his cowcatcher nose.

One desire obsessed him: to repair his nose. But that took money. Since the death of Dr. Estabrook no plastic surgeon practiced at Mercy Hospital. The only solution was to go to a plastic surgeon in private practice, but that was far beyond Cowcatcher Nose's means.

Inevitably it occurred to him to steal the money. One night he tied a handkerchief over his face and went out and held up a gas station. Unfortunately it was a windy night. A gust of wind blew the handkerchief off his face as he was fleeing the station. This enabled the gas station attendant to supply a most graphic description to the police when they arrived a few moments later. Cowcatcher Nose was quickly apprehended, convicted, and sent to prison.

During his journey to prison, he thought things over. He realized that he had been mistaken in turning to crime. He made up his mind that after he had paid his debt to society he would thenceforth live a normal, useful life in spite of his disfigurement. Perhaps he could learn a trade in prison, find a good job after his release, save his money, and maybe someday be able to afford a new nose. Cowcatcher Nose was actually feeling good as he entered the prison gates.

As was the custom at this prison, he was taken to the office of the warden immediately after his admittance. The warden, who was curiously enough also named Scott, gave Cowcatcher Nose his usual lecture to incoming convicts. In this case he delivered his speech more rapidly than usual, for, being a highborn, fastidious man, the sight of Cowcatcher Nose's nose was disturbing to him and he wished to get him out of the office as soon as possible.

"Are there any questions?" asked the warden when he had finished his orientation.

"As a matter of fact, there are," replied Cowcatcher Nose. "I notice that your name is Scott too. I wonder if we could be related."

"Certainly not," replied the warden with a shudder.

"I don't know," persisted Cowcatcher Nose. "You look a lot like a great-uncle of mine."

"Guard," called the warden. "Throw this man in solitary."

Cowcatcher Nose was forthwith placed in an oubliette where he remained for six weeks. After this period he was transferred to a cell and allowed to participate in the normal activities of the prison. This meant that he could write one letter a month. His first letter was to his parents, asking many questions of a genealogical nature. For during his solitary confinement Cowcatcher Nose had become convinced that he and the warden were indeed related.

A reply came from his parents a week later, detailing his antecedents and corollary branches of the family for several generations back. Sure enough, Cowcatcher Nose discovered that Warden Scott was a cross-cousin of a nephew of his great-aunt.

Cowcatcher Nose acquainted the warden with this intelligence one afternoon when the warden was inspecting the jute mill. "Ridiculous," snapped the warden, reddening. "I'll have you know that I'm a direct descendant of Sir Walter Scott."

"Come on up to my cell and I'll show you the letter," said Cowcatcher Nose.

The warden declined the invitation and instead had Cowcatcher Nose returned to solitary for another six weeks. But Cowcatcher Nose clung to his idea, and as soon as he was able to write letters again, he inquired of his parents whether Sir Walter Scott was among their progenitors.

He received an affirmative reply. Moreover, said his mother and father, they—and Cowcatcher Nose too—were members of the Kenilworth Society, an organization composed exclusively of descendants of Sir Walter Scott. Each year the Kenilworth Society held an outing on the banks of Loch Ness, and each year Cowcatcher Nose's parents received an invitation to come over for a day of jousting and alfresco supper. Because of the expense involved in such a trip, they naturally had to decline. They explained that they had never mentioned these invitations to Cowcatcher Nose before because they had not wanted him to be disappointed at not being able to attend.

Cowcatcher Nose could hardly wait until he saw the warden again. His first opportunity was at a softball game between the Arsonists and the Breakers-and-Enterers. During the seventh-inning stretch, Cowcatcher Nose raced to the warden's side and told him all about his membership in the Kenilworth Society. Again the warden grew angry and ordered Cowcatcher Nose committed to solitary.

"All right!" shouted Cowcatcher Nose as the guards dragged him away. "Just you wait and see. As soon as I get out of this prison, I'm going to go over to Scotland and go to one of those outings. And you can't stop me, either!"

Cowcatcher Nose had occasion later to regret this defiant statement. As it happened, the warden was in the habit of attending the annual Kenilworth Society outings at Loch Ness. He was, in fact, the only American to attend. At these outings, the warden knew, one found the very cream of British and Scottish society, many of them titled, all of them keen scholars of heraldry. The warden himself, wellborn though he was, had been regarded as a parvenu for a long time. Only after many years did the other members become satisfied that he was a gentleman and accept him wholeheartedly.

The warden was appalled at the thought of Cowcatcher Nose attending a Kenilworth Society outing. How would they feel when they saw this great boor with his unthinkable nose? After their initial horror they would certainly vote to disaffiliate the American branch of the Kenilworth Society. The warden gnashed his teeth. He had come to look forward with great zest to these annual outings.

He must, he decided, prevent Cowcatcher Nose from attending. But how? Obviously he had a right to attend. Well, thought the warden grimly, if he could not prevent Cowcatcher Nose's attendance, he could at least delay it; he could see to it that no parole shortened Cowcatcher Nose's ten-year sentence.

So when after five years Cowcatcher Nose became eligible for parole, the warden sent his application to the parole board with a negative endorsement. And he did the same with all subsequent applications.

The warden's spitefulness only served to strengthen Cowcatcher Nose's determination. He was going to go to the Kenilworth Society outing and nothing could stop him. Through ten long years he thought of nothing else. He performed his prison tasks automatically, he eschewed conversation with his fellow inmates, he ate his meals without tasting. During his rare leisure periods he went to the prison library and read the few volumes of Sir Walter

Scott's novels which were there, read them and reread them until he had them committed to memory.

When at last his time was up, Cowcatcher Nose was called into the warden's office to receive his discharge. "Listen," said the warden with a nervous smile, "you're not really going to the Kenilworth Society outing, are you?"

"Yes," said Cowcatcher Nose quietly. "Yes, I am, Cousin."

At this the warden flew into a towering rage and toppled over, dead of apoplexy.

When he got back to the city, Cowcatcher Nose went to a secondhand bookstore and bought the complete works of Sir Walter Scott. Then he found a shack on the edge of town and sat down and read all the books three times. After that he began to make his plans.

Forgotten now was his ten-year-old resolution to go straight. He needed a lot of money in a hurry, and only crime would provide it. "I might as well," he told himself, "steal enough to get my nose fixed too, so I will look nice at the outing."

This, then, could be no petty robbery. It had to be big. A bank would do, but one needed an organization for this type work. For safecracking one needed equipment. It had to be something that a lone man could do with his bare hands. In a little while the answer came to him: kidnaping.

He scouted the town for several weeks, looking for a likely kidnaping prospect. Finally he settled on the family of Daniel Mainwaring. Mr. Mainwaring was the town's leading real-estate dealer. He had a fortune of several million dollars, and boy and girl twins, aged nine. Cowcatcher Nose decided to kidnap just one of the twins instead of both. "Mr. Mainwaring will pay just as much for one as for both," he thought. "He won't want to break up a set."

So one moonless night Cowcatcher Nose slipped through the window of the Mainwaring nursery, threw a blanket over the boy, and carried him off to his shack. In the boy's bed he left a note demanding $100,000 in ransom.

The boy, whose name was Marvin, slept all through his abduction. When he woke in Cowcatcher Nose's shack, he made no outcry. In fact, he seemed rather pleased to be there. The truth was that Marvin was delighted to get away from his twin sister Esther because she pinched him all the time.

Esther had good reason for pinching Marvin, or at least she thought she did. Esther's hair was straight and stringy; Marvin's was thick, soft, and curly. People always used to say, "It's too bad that he wasn't the girl and she wasn't the boy." These comments caused Esther to hate her twin brother, and that is why she pinched him.

On the morning after Marvin's kidnaping Esther woke early and went over to pinch her brother. She saw the ransom note lying in his bed. She read the note and broke into a huge grin. "If I tear up the note," she thought exultantly, "they won't know where he is and I will be rid of him." She destroyed the note instanter. Later, when her parents asked her where Marvin was, she shook her head innocently and replied, "Damn if I know."

Meanwhile, in Cowcatcher Nose's shack, Marvin was enjoying himself thoroughly. Cowcatcher Nose had opened a can of beans for breakfast and now he was reading aloud from *Quentin Durward.* Marvin listened with shining eyes, delighted at not being pinched and loving Sir Walter Scott's romantic tale. At noon they had another can of beans, and then Cowcatcher Nose read until evening. At nightfall Cowcatcher Nose went out to inspect the hollow tree where he had instructed Mr. Mainwaring to leave the ransom money. There was nothing there. He returned to the shack, opened another can of beans, and then read until bedtime.

The next day he read *Ivanhoe.* There was nothing in the hollow tree that night. The day after that he read *Rob Roy.* Again there was nothing in the tree. That night, as he tucked Marvin in, he said, "I think I better send another letter. Maybe they didn't find the first one."

"Aw, gee, Cowcatcher Nose, do you *have* to?" asked Marvin. "I don't want to go home. It's such fun being here with you and listening to all those wonderful stories."

"They are fine stories, aren't they?" said Cowcatcher Nose with a smile.

"They sure are," agreed Marvin.

"You know, I'm a descendant of Sir Walter Scott."

"Gee," said Marvin.

"Well, all right," said Cowcatcher Nose. "I'll wait till tomorrow. But if I don't get an answer by then, I'm going to write another letter."

The next day he read *The Heart of Midlothian,* and the

tree was still empty. Waving aside the boy's protests, he wrote a second letter demanding $100,000 and posted it.

Esther, suspecting that another letter would follow, was waiting when the postman arrived. She intercepted the letter and burned it when her parents were not looking.

In the next several days Cowcatcher Nose read *The Bride of Lammermoor, The Legend of Montrose, The Two Drovers,* and *The Fortunes of Nigel.* When he still did not receive a reply to his letter, he began to think that perhaps he was asking too much ransom. He wrote another letter, reducing his demand to $75,000. This letter, like the others, was intercepted by Esther and destroyed.

The days passed with the reading of *Guy Mannering, The Antiquary, The Black Dwarf, The Abbot, The Pirate,* and *Peveril of the Peak.* Still the hollow tree remained empty. To make matters worse, the stock of canned beans was running low and Cowcatcher Nose had no money to buy more. He put himself on half rations, but continued to give Marvin his full share. Marvin noticed this and protested.

"Yea and verily," said Marvin, "if food is not a-plenty, then let me also do without. Zounds!"

"Nay," smiled Cowcatcher Nose, patting Marvin's curly head. "Thou art a growing knight. I pray thee, say no more."

That night Cowcatcher Nose wrote a letter cutting the ransom to $50,000. When he received no reply after reading *Marmion, Kenilworth, St. Ronan's Well,* and *Lady of the Lake,* he lowered the ransom further to $25,000. *Red-*

gauntlet and *The Talisman* were read when he made the ransom $10,000. After *The Betrothed* and *The Surgeon's Daughter* he cut to $5,000.

By this time Marvin was reading aloud to Cowcatcher Nose, for Cowcatcher Nose was too weak with hunger to read any more. Only a few cans of beans remained, and these were carefully husbanded for the boy in spite of his protests.

"Sirrah," cried Marvin, much concerned, "thou appearst not well to me. Thou betterst eat something."

But Cowcatcher Nose only smiled and patted the boy's head.

Marvin read *Anne of Geierstein* and *Auchindrane,* and Cowcatcher Nose reduced the ransom to $1000. It dropped to $500 after *Tales of the Crusaders,* $250 after *Count Robert of Paris,* $100 after *Vision of Don Roderick,* and $50 after *Tales of a Grandfather.*

One afternoon while Marvin was reading *Castle Dangerous,* Cowcatcher Nose stopped suddenly in the middle of writing a letter asking for $1.50. He felt the last of his strength ebbing out of him, and he knew that the end was at hand. "Farewell, fair knight," he said to Marvin. Then he closed his eyes forever.

Marvin sat quietly for a long time. At length he rose and walked out of the shack and back to his own home.

What a hue and cry greeted him there! His mother wept, his father wept, his sister pinched him, photographers took pictures, reporters and policemen fired questions, everyone shouted and shoved. Marvin stood quietly through all this uproar, a slight smile on his lips, a curious look in his eyes.

Finally everyone fell quiet. "Where," asked Mr. Mainwaring, "have you been?"

"I have been," said Marvin, fending off his sister, "on a journey to the past—to the days of chivalry and jousts and mortal combat, of knights in armor and damsels in distress, of castles and white chargers and heraldic trumpets, of lances and battle-axes . . . I shall never forget it."

Nor did he ever forget it. When Mr. Mainwaring died and Marvin inherited the real-estate business, the very first thing he did was to build an entire suburb in the form of a medieval village. Each house had plastic battlements on the roof, a tile-lined moat in front, an electronically operated drawbridge over the moat, and a neon coat of arms on the front door. Although the other realtors in town laughed at Marvin and called him a romantic dreamer, he made a profit of three and a half million dollars on Ivanhoe Gardens, as he named the development.

This is where Esme Geddes lived.

CHAPTER 6

It was with some misgivings that I crossed the moat to Esme Geddes's door. This was, so to speak, my debut into society. How, I wondered, would I acquit myself? My previous social experience had been entirely with people of low estate, boors and vulgarians whose idea of pleasure was to drink whisky and sing raucous ballads and neck. This sort of thing, I thought with a wry smile, had scarcely prepared me for one of Miss Geddes's soirees.

I stood hesitantly on the stoop. Inside the door were tycoons and littérateurs, captains of finance and industry, legislators, sportsmen, artists, eminent members of the professions. What had I to offer this distinguished company? A pleasant disposition, yes. An ingratiating personality, yes. A good heart, an alert mind, sympathy, understanding, intelligence, loyalty, honesty—all these things, yes. But that was not enough. In this glittering gathering one needed also to be attractive, quick, amusing. And was I?

Well, was I not?

Perhaps I could not be called handsome in the ordinary sense, being rather too bulletheaded to conform to the popular conception of good looks. Nevertheless, I was attractive to many women, particularly women interested in ballistics.

As a conversationalist I was not without ability. In repartee I had always given as good as I received. "Oh yeah?" I would say in a duel of cutting remarks, or sometimes "Sez you!" when the situation called for an especially acerb retort. When a philosophical observation was indicated, I would say "That's life" or "That's the way it goes," depending on which seemed more appropriate. I also improvised humorous remarks for special occasions and was known in some quarters as "a regular Bob Hope."

As a parlor entertainer my repertory was limited, but what I did I did well. I will wager that I imitated Lionel Barrymore far better than he could have imitated me.

All in all I had a quite respectable inventory of social assets. Besides which I had a pleasant disposition, an ingratiating personality, a good heart, an alert mind, sympathy, understanding intelligence, loyalty, and honesty. Truly I had no cause to worry about making a good impression on Miss Geddes's guests. All I had to do was to come in with a warm smile and a kind word, to be charming, gallant, gay, and witty—in short, to be myself. Confidently I pressed the doorbell.

To the distinguished-looking young woman who answered the doorbell I gave a warm smile and a kind word. "My dear," I said, "what a chic dress!"

"Thanks, mister," she replied, blushing with pleasure. "It's the latest thing in maid's uniforms. These here pockets in the apron are for canapés."

"Chic," I murmured again and handed her my cap and went into the living room.

How shall I describe the scene that greeted me there? Eh? I had known, of course, that the upper classes had a talent for relaxation, but I had not imagined that they could be *that* relaxed. Some, in fact, were quite unconscious. But most of them were relaxing vertically or diagonally. Some relaxed at the bar, consuming quantities of the fine spirits that are such an important part of gracious living. Some relaxed around the piano, singing a hellishly clever ditty entitled "Roll Me Over." Some relaxed in pairs on divans and demonstrated the affection they bore each other. What a difference, I thought, between the gentility of this party and the disgusting drunken orgies in which the lower classes foregathered.

I wandered about the room with a warm smile until I spied my hostess over in a corner. I went immediately to her, pausing on my way to tell a well-dressed gentleman, "My dear, what a chic suit!"

Miss Geddes was balancing a fish bowl on her head when I reached her. I waited politely until she had completed her trick and the maid had swept up the broken glass and dead fish before I made my hello. "Good evening, my dear," I said. "What a chic party!"

"Wipe me off," said Miss Geddes.

"Wipe me off," said Miss Geddes.

"Delighted," I murmured. I wiped her spirally from her collarbone to her *sphincter ani,* trying desperately as I sloshed off water and bits of kelp to control the excitement which her proximity awoke within me. Faint though I was with desire, I knew that a breach of decorum would forever estrange her from me, and this I should not be able to abide.

"Now if I had some brushes," I said with a warm smile, "I could curry you."

"Go get me a drink," said Miss Geddes. "No soda."

"Honored," I breathed. I elbowed my way to the bar and returned with a glass of fine spirits. She drained it in one delicate draught.

"Who the hell are you?" she asked, looking at me narrowly.

"Surely you remember," I replied with a warm smile. "I'm Harry Riddle."

"Oh yes." She stopped a distinguished-looking woman who was walking past. "Harriet," she said, "this is the pauper I was telling you about."

I lowered my eyes modestly.

"Hm," said the woman, with the perfectly concealed interest which is the mark of true breeding.

"You're Harriet and I'm Harry. Quite a coincidence," I said with a warm smile.

"Is it?" she said and walked away before I had a chance to tell her how chic her dress was.

"Charming woman," I said to Miss Geddes.

"Go get me a drink," she replied. "No soda."

I was back in a moment with another glass of spirits. "Your drink, madame," I said, bending over in a courtly bow and spilling the spirits on the floor. "No matter," I chuckled. "I'll fetch another."

When I returned Miss Geddes was dancing with a well-dressed gentleman of distinguished mien. I followed them around the floor with the drink, knowing that Miss Geddes would be thirsty when she completed the dance. They ground their bodies together in a modish two-step I had not previously seen and then went through a pair of french doors to a handsome flagstone terrace. I followed with the drink. They sat down on a glider and proceeded to kiss one another with great good nature. Old friends, I assumed, and, not wishing to intrude, withdrew behind a potted palm.

In a short while a woman in a chic dress appeared, scratched Miss Geddes, and took the young man away, leading him by one finger crooked under his upper lip. I was sure it was all a misunderstanding but, not knowing the details, was unable to help clear it up. All I could do was to offer Miss Geddes her drink with a warm smile. She threw it in my face and walked away.

Chuckling at her exuberance, I went back into the living room to mingle with the guests. With things going so well for me, my original timidity about meeting all these high-type people had quite vanished. With great self-assurance I walked up to a portly, distinguished-looking gentleman and introduced myself. "How do you do? I'm Harry Riddle."

"Unions," he said.

"Sir?" I said.

"Mind you," he said, "I'm not a union baiter."

"I daresay you're not," I daresaid.

"Do you think," he asked, "that I object because they're getting tremendous wages for no work?"

"Well——" I said.

"Or because they're all controlled by Red Russia?"

"I——" I said.

"Or because they're destroying free private enterprise, which is the very foundation of this great country?"

"Sir," I said, "one could scarcely blame you if you objected."

"Ah," he exclaimed, prodding my thorax with his forefinger, "but I don't! *That* isn't what I object to."

"What, then?" I asked, consumed with curiosity.

"They've dehumanized business, that's what," he declared. "They've taken all the warm personal relations out of industry."

"That's the way it goes," I observed.

"It used to be," he continued, "when I wanted to fire a man, I would call him into my office and give him the sack, man to man. But now—shop stewards, grievance committees, red tape. It's so cold and mechanical."

He sighed, and so did I to put him at his ease.

"And Christmas," he said. "That's what I miss most of all—those old-fashioned Christmases. In the old days I would visit every one of my workers' houses personally and hand him a Christmas basket. Wearing heavy gloves, of course." He blinked back a tear.

"Sweet," I said. Here was a simple, sentimental man who was living negation of all the lies one hears about hard-hearted capitalists. I felt that I should like to know him better, but he turned his back abruptly and opened a conversation with someone else—with his own reflection in a mirror, actually—and I wandered away.

I approached a stately, distinguished-looking lady and introduced myself with a warm smile.

"Gas," she said.

"Ma'am?" I said.

"Gas on my stomach."

"I'm sorry," I said.

"Burning sensation under my heart." She tapped her diaphragm. "Coated tongue." She showed me.

"Vertigo?" I asked.

She nodded.

"Hm," I said.

"Acid condition," she said. "Dull, logy, under-par."

"Have you made a will?" I asked.

"No."

"I'm an attorney," I said, seeing no harm in combining business with pleasure.

"No use making a will," she replied. "You can't leave alimony."

"Oh, then you're divorced."

She belched affirmatively.

"How chic! Would you care to tell me about it?"

"He sued," she said. "Told the judge that I denied him a husband's privileges. But I couldn't help it."

"Gas?" I asked.

She nodded.

"That's life," I said.

"First divorce case on record," she said, walking away, "where a duodenum was named as correspondent."

I crossed the room to a tall, distinguished-looking gentleman. "I'm Harry Riddle," I said. "How do you do?"

"Maxfield Parrish," he replied.

"Pleased to meet you, Mr. Parrish."

He frowned. "I was referring to the blue of the Mexican sky. You've been, of course."

"Well, no."

He took a sheaf of photographs from his breast pocket. "My wife and I at Oaxaca," he said, handing me a picture.

"Handsome woman," I remarked.

"You're holding it upside down."

I righted the photo and looked again. "She's not so handsome at that," I said.

"Ugly as sin." He gave me another picture. "Here we are at Sabancuy. That's Pedro, our Mexican guide."

"He seems very devoted to you," I said.

"Stole my car and all my clothes," he said.

"A gentle, carefree people," I said.

He handed me another picture. "Fiesta at Zacatecas."

"What volcano is that in the background?"

"That's my wife in a sombrero," he said.

"Oh," I said.

"How long were you in Mexico?" he asked.

"You misunderstand," I said. "I never——"

"Didn't you love San Luis Potosi?" he said. "That funny little bridge there? I understand some fellow wrote a book about it."

"But I never——"

"Do you remember that crazy little café at Tuxpan where they served iguanaburgers?"

"But——"

"I see you've got pictures. May I?" He took back his pictures and examined them. "Terrible focus. What kind of camera do you have?"

"A brownie," I said. "I made it myself."

"This woman at the fiesta," he said, "looks a little like my wife. I must show you my pictures sometime. We'll have lunch at your club."

"They don't serve lunch at the Settlement House," I said. "Sometimes they have hot dogs when there's a basketball game."

"Hasta la vista," he said as he walked away.

"Blasco ibáñez," I replied. I know a little Spanish.

I continued my circuit of the room, moving from one conversation to another, each as rewarding as the last. After I had spoken to all the guests, a few of whom had replied to me, I asked Miss Geddes whether I might take a look around the house. "I don't give a good goddam," she answered. Taking this cryptic statement for affirmation, I thanked her and proceeded to make a leisurely tour of the house.

I had seen well-appointed rooms before—in furniture stores—but I was not prepared for the magnificence I now encountered. Wide-eyed with wonder, I went from one splendid chamber to the next, tiptoeing quietly in the bedrooms so as not to disturb the guests taking their pleasure there. What lovely things I saw—damask tablecloths, sterling silver, Sèvres china, rugs from Trebizond, Chippendale chairs, Duncan Phyfe escritoires, flush toilets.

I was filled with admiration—but more than admiration. There was an acute longing in my breast—a longing for a home like this, for appointments like these, for a life such as all the people led whom I had met this night. How fine it would be to be well-housed, well-clothed, well-fed, to be urbane and polished. How splendid to live graciously.

And why shouldn't I? I had all the graces. All I lacked was money. I'll get it, I thought with a surge of determination. I hammered my fist into my palm. I'll get money, no matter what!

Suddenly I was gripped by a cold fear, horrified at the savagery of my determination. I'll get money, no matter what, I had thought. *No matter what!* Could I truly have meant that? Was I so covetous of wealth that I would not shrink from any means of obtaining it? Would I sacrifice principle, integrity, and honesty for money? Would I? Faint, I sank weakly into a chair.

Money corrupts. Somebody had said that to me long ago. Who? Ah, I remembered. The young man at the cafeteria where I had worked—the intense young man who read big, fat books and worried about the world. What was his name? George Overmeyer, that was it.

Money corrupts, George had told me back in my busboy days, and I had been sorely troubled by his statement. But I had decided that by becoming a lawyer I would avoid the danger of corruption. Obviously it hadn't worked. If the very thought of money could arouse such passion in me—"I'll get money, no matter what"—then I stood in mortal peril of being corrupted. Clearly the only way for me to remain pure was to remain a pauper. It was a hard prospect, but there was no other way to preserve my integrity. That was the important thing—preserving my integrity.

But perhaps I was being hasty. Did money *always* corrupt? Certainly the character of the man who had the money needed to be taken into account. Money would corrupt a weak man, yes—a mean man, yes. But weak men and mean men were not being considered here. I was the case in point—I, a strong man, a generous man, a man of intelligence, sensitivity, perspicacity, insight, and penetration. Could a man such as I be corrupted? The idea was ridiculous.

I rose from the chair feeling vastly relieved. A great boulder had been removed from my path. Now with good heart and clear conscience I would go forth and get rich. And I would succeed, by Godfrey! I'd get money, no matter what——

There was that horrendous thought again. I fell back into the chair. Oh, what a confusion! What a perplexity! And there was nobody I could turn to for advice. Talking to Dad would not help. Wise as he was, he was inclined to oversimplify when it came to money. He thought any way you got it was all right. I have heard him speak highly of Dillinger.

If only I knew where George Overmeyer was. There was someone who could tell me what to do. All those books he had read, all those hours he had pondered—surely he had the answer to my question. But where was he?

Sighing, I rose from the chair. I would just have to figure things out for myself. But later, not now. Now I had to return to Miss Geddes's party. They were all probably very agitated about my long absence.

I started down the expensive staircase.

CHAPTER 7

The guests must have despaired at my returning and gone home, for when I got back to the living room only three people remained: Miss Geddes and a distinguished-looking young woman who sat on the divan silently passing a brandy bottle back and forth, and over at the piano a distinguished-looking young man who stood picking out the "Funeral March" with two fingers.

"Hello, hello, hello," I cried cheerily and went over to the ladies with a broad smile. They looked up at me slowly.

"Who the hell are you?" asked Miss Geddes.

"Harry Riddle," I chuckled. Little minx.

They looked down again and resumed passing the bottle. I stood watching them—watching Miss Geddes, actually, for although the other lady was most attractive, my eyes were only for my hostess. Miss Geddes sat utterly relaxed, totally unguarded. A wave of tenderness swept over me. How like a child she looked in repose! How like a child's her sweet, tired face! How like a child's her soft white throat! Below that the resemblance ended.

My eyes were only for my hostess.

Both Miss Geddes and the other lady seemed disinclined to speak, so after standing over them for a little while—hardly more than an hour—I went across the room to visit with the young man at the piano. He seemed familiar, but I did not recognize him at once. He was much heavier than when I had last seen him; his cheeks had filled out and the eyes that used to blaze were now somnolent in their little pockets of fat. It took a full minute before I knew who he was.

Then, "George!" I cried. "George Overmeyer!"

For it was he. A kind fate had brought him to me when I needed him most.

"George! George! George!" I kept repeating as I pumped his hand.

"Hello, Harry," he said. "So you made it too."

"Made what?"

"The middle class."

I smiled wryly. "I'm afraid not. Not yet, at any rate. . . . But you—have you made it?"

He nodded. "America," he said simply.

I grasped him by the shoulders and looked into his eyes. "Tell me, George, are you corrupted?"

"Mercy me, no," he replied. "I am daily nobler."

"Oh, happy day!" I cried joyously. My worries were over; money did not corrupt. Now, without reservations, I could begin the long, painful climb to riches.

"Tell me about your long, painful climb to riches," I said.

"I married it," said George.

I looked at the young woman on the divan beside Miss Geddes.

George nodded.

"Chic," I murmured.

"Damn right. Owns the chic-est liquor store you ever saw. That is, *we* own it."

"Hm," I mused. "Somehow I can't see you running a liquor store."

"Not many people do. I get there in the afternoon, pick up some booze, take the money out of the till, and blow. Makes a nice short day."

"What do you do with the rest of the day?"

"Well, I sleep till noon . . ."

(Dad's words came back to me. Wise, wise Dad.)

". . . and then an expensive servant serves my expensive breakfast. Then I drop in at the store to pick up some liquor and money. Then I take my wife to the track and lose the money. In the evenings we get drunk."

"Beats working," I chuckled. "Now tell me all about the middle class."

"You've come to the right man," he said. "I am the world's greatest authority on the middle class since Sinclair Lewis gave it up in favor of octoroons."

I sat down cross-legged on the floor and cupped my hands over my ears, the better to hear.

George began: "It is a mistake to think that the bourgeoisie are motivated by a desire for wealth. This kind of thinking overlooks the heart of the matter. When Bourgeois Jones buys a new car even though his old car is still perfectly serviceable, he is not doing it simply because he himself wants a new car. He is doing it primarily so that his neighbors Smith and Green and Brown will see his new car and admire it. It is for *them* that he buys the car. It is for their wives that Mrs. Jones buys a new gown. Mr. and Mrs. Jones do not do things for themselves, but for others. In short, the bourgeoisie are motivated by *love.*"

"Of course," I cried. "Why didn't I see that before?"

"Ah, then you agree?"

"Yes. Oh yes."

"I thought you would," said George. "The ignorance I detected in you as a youth has now crystallized into a limitless capacity for rationalization."

"Thank you." I was grateful that the lamps had all been broken and he could not see my blush.

"Perhaps you have a future after all. There *have* been cases of idiocy turned to advantage."

I could not but thank him again.

"You're welcome. Where was I?"

"You and I were agreeing that the bourgeoisie are motivated by love."

"Oh yes. Now, you and I know this is true. It is possible, however, to hold another view. Some might think that our Mr. Jones buys a new car to make his neighbors wretched with envy, not because he loves them. It is also possible to make unflattering allegations about how Mr. Jones got the money to buy the car in the first place. Communists, for instance, might have something to say on this subject."

"Why don't they go back where they came from?" I snarled.

"Because they came from nowhere. Communism is from

nowhere. It's a crock. Aside from its obvious unattractiveness—I mean things like murder and slavery—it has no intellectual substance. It's based on a denial of the first human principle: self. It's a nonesuch—a bubble and a chimera. It's repugnant to a thinking man."

"And to me too," I said.

"Of course you can have a low opinion of the bourgeoisie and not be a communist. You could be, for example, a Jeffersonian Democrat or a Lincolnian Republican . . . or a Christian."

"Well, George," I said, clapping his back, "you've certainly relieved my mind. I can't tell you how happy I am to know that money can't corrupt anybody."

"But it can," said George.

I bit my lip in anguish, and George hastened to reassure me. "Not you and me, of course. We, with our massive intellects, can handle the stuff. But let's talk about a couple of other fellows—hypothetical fellows. They both start out poor and uncorrupted—I better stop here and emphasize that poor and uncorrupted are not synonymous. Some of the meanest sons of bitches I know haven't got a pot. In any class a good man is hard to find.

"But let's get back to our two hypothetical boys. They both start out poor and uncorrupted. One is smart; one is dumb. The smart one knows there is something wrong with the world. What's more, he knows what it is: man's inhumanity to man. As a pauper, our smart boy is engaged in two fights. The primary—and more urgent—fight is simply the struggle to earn a living. The second fight is to improve the world. He's carrying on both fights at once, and he's getting his brains knocked out. Then suddenly, somehow, he comes into a lot of money."

"Possibly he marries a rich girl," I suggested.

"A brilliant idea."

I squirmed with pleasure.

"He marries a rich girl and now the first fight is won. There is no more worrying about money; he's set up in a thriving business and the loot is pouring in. Now he can devote all his energy to the second fight—to improve the world. But he doesn't."

"How come?"

"Because when he had to fight for a living he was a man in motion, and he had enough impetus to carry him into a second fight. But now the initial push—the need to earn a living—is gone. Inertia sets in. He tells himself that the fight to improve the world is hopeless—and don't think an airtight case can't be made for such an opinion. Why should he stir himself for a lost cause? So he gives up *all* fighting altogether and devotes himself to peace, pleasure, and alcohol."

I brushed aside a tear. "Lost, lorn man," I sighed.

"Now let's examine our second hypothetical man—the dope. He doesn't know there's anything wrong with the world. He thinks it's jim-dandy, and he loves everybody. His only struggle is to make a living—aggravated in his case by imbecility. Then suddenly he comes into money."

"Let's have him marry a rich girl too, huh, George?"

"By all means. He, too, is set up in a thriving business.

Two Hypothetical Boys

Now, two things can happen—both bad. First, he can lose all his money through his stupidity. That's bad because he'll never again be happy poor. Before, as a benign imbecile, he had, at least, been harmless. But now, as a bitter imbecile, the mind trembles at what could happen to him."

My mind trembled.

"But let's explore the second possibility. Let's say that he survives in business. Here, now, is what will happen. The essence of business is competition. In competition one man hurts another man. Our sweet dope is going to start hurting people. And it won't be just the superficial bruises of normal commerce. With his sense of proportion, this knothead will absolutely *massacre* people. And on top of it, he'll be able to persuade himself that he's doing them a favor. The world's champion rationalizer, this one."

"Lost, lorn man," I sighed.

"Now let me review what I've been saying."

"No, no, let *me*," I urged, and George graciously consented. "Your argument breaks down into three main points," I said. "Number One: money can corrupt smart people. Number Two: money can corrupt dumb people. Number Three: money can't corrupt us."

"Masterful," said George.

"I was a whiz at this kind of stuff in school," I confessed with lowered eyes.

"What time is it?" he asked.

I pulled out my Mickey Mouse watch. "Twelve-thirty."

"Good. It's a new day. I can start drinking again. I've made it a rule never to take more than a quart in one day."

"Sensible," I said and accompanied him to the bar, where he filled a glass from a flagon of fine spirits. As George drank I stood thinking. Now that he had dispelled my doubts about getting rich, nothing further barred my way. All that remained was to do it, and there on the spot I so resolved.

"George," I said, "I'm going to get rich. I'm going to have fine clothes and drive a big car and live in Ivanhoe Gardens and marry a distinguished-looking girl."

He inclined his head toward Miss Geddes, who sat tilting a brandy bottle on the divan. "Her?"

I reddened. "Oh no."

"Don't you want her?"

"More than anything in the world. But she is so delicate and sensitive and pure, and I"—I shrugged—"well, I'm pretty delicate, sensitive, and pure myself. But nowhere," I added quickly, "as delicate, sensitive, and pure as she."

George finished his drink and poured another. "Harry, isn't there some nice girl in your neighborhood?"

"In *my* neighborhood? You know better than that."

"Well, in the general vicinity."

"Conceivably. Why?"

"Go find her and marry her and get a good union job someplace and forget about getting rich."

"What? And spend the rest of my life with boors and dullards? No, George, not after tonight."

"You liked the Ivanhoe Gardens set?"

"Who would not?"

"Let me tell you a little about them."

Me cross-legged on the floor again, hands cupped over ears.

"The leader of Ivanhoe Gardens society, by virtue of having the most money, is a man named Payson Atterbury. He wasn't here tonight. He was out repossessing cars."

What an odd hobby, I thought, but politely held my tongue.

He continued: "Atterbury is a moneylender. 'The Great Forecloser,' some call him. He specializes in bad risks. When people are in trouble and the banks won't help them, they know they can always go to Atterbury. He has boundless faith in people. No matter what the banks think of them as risks, Atterbury is willing to take a chance, and his interest rates often run below 100 per cent. In the matter of collateral he is also much more liberal than the banks. He will, for example, accept such things as gold inlays, relatives, or prosthetic devices."

"A greathearted man," I said.

"And perfectly mated. His wife goes around looking for people who need Atterbury's aid. In fact, she is often instrumental in reducing them to that condition."

"A greathearted woman," I said.

"Atterbury is the leader of this set. Around him are a dozen or so retailers, factors, jobbers, and professionals—charming people all. The days are gone when a middle-class businessman was a Babbitt. These men are sons of Babbitts, yes, but they themselves—although not lacking their fathers' acumen—have much more rounded-out personalities. They read all the latest book digests and news capsules. At their weekly fraternal lunches they hear erudite but dynamic speakers who fill them in on such topics as 'If Freud Were in the Ready-to-Wear Line' and 'Toynbee and Inventories.' They are the enlightened generation of businessmen.

"The women of Ivanhoe Gardens," continued George, "bear a relationship to their husbands roughly resembling that of a jockey to a horse. In this race the horses happen to be as intent on winning as the jockeys, but sometimes a horse may flag or stray. When this happens, the jockey is quick to apply the whip. A certain piquancy is added to the race by the fact that the jockeys occasionally switch horses."

I must confess that all these turf terms bewildered me. I know a few things about racing: that a furlong is a mile and a quarter, that a stud fee is what you put in the pari-mutuel machine, that a horse must be a citizen to run in the Kentucky Derby. Beyond that, however, my knowledge is blank. But I didn't want to interrupt George with questions, so I just nodded.

He reached over and rubbed my head. "Trying to get information to you," he said, "is like trying to shove an oyster into a keyhole."

The significance of the simile escaped me, but it made a funny picture. I laughed silverly.

"Ah, nuts," said George, suddenly gloomy. "It's my own fault. Why must I talk to you in goddam circles? Why can't I say what I mean in plain English?"

He finished his drink and poured another. "I know why,"

he said. "Because I haven't got an argument. What am I going to tell you—that poverty is noble? Poverty stinks. So does this, but at least you're comfortable. Get rich, Harry. I can't imagine how you'll do it, but do it."

"Thank you," I cried, leaping to my feet. "That's what I wanted to hear you say."

George's head sank slowly to the bar. "Yes, Harry, get rich," he mumbled. "You won't even need liquor to keep from thinking." His eyes closed and he began to snore lightly.

I looked over at the ladies on the sofa, thinking perhaps they might now be desirous of conversation. But they were busy, engaged in some kind of nautical game. Miss Geddes was holding the brandy bottle to her eye, telescope fashion, and crying, "Thar she blows!" The other lady lay on her back ejecting jets of water from her mouth. I chuckled at their genteel antics.

Then suddenly I grew speculative. I turned to the sleeping George. Here was a man with the same humble origins as my own. He was no more attractive, no more accomplished, no more poised than I. Then I turned to the distinguished-looking, well-bred lady spitting water on the sofa. How, I wondered, did George ever capture such a prize?

I turned back to George and shook him awake. "George," I said, "tell me about your courtship."

George blinked a few times and poured himself another drink. "Glad to," he said. "Agnes and I had what you might call a whirlwind romance. I first met her at a party at her house. I should point out that I was not a guest. At this time I was working in her father's liquor store, and I had been pressed into service as a bartender at this party. It was quite a party. There were all kinds of ingenious diversions. Damage ran into the thousands. By dawn all the guests had passed out or gone home, but Agnes was still in a mood for frolic. 'You there,' she said to me—she knew my name but preferred this more correct form of address —'you there, let's have some fun.'

" 'What would you like to do, ma'am?' I asked politely.

" 'Think of something, stupid,' she replied.

" 'There are a few windows still unbroken,' I suggested.

" 'Balls,' she replied.

" 'How about turning in some false alarms?' I suggested.

" 'Balls,' she replied.

"She made the same circular observation about several more of my suggestions. 'Always the same old crap,' she said peevishly. 'Can't you think of anything *new?*'

"At this point I had an inspiration. 'Have you ever been married?' I asked.

"She perked up immediately, and the next thing I knew we were on our way to a justice of the peace."

"It's like a storybook romance," I breathed.

But George was not listening. He was running rapidly across the room. Miss Geddes, still playing the whaling game, had her arm drawn back and was taking careful aim on Mrs. Overmeyer with a brass fireplace poker. George seized the poker just as it was about to fly from her hand.

"Shoddy goddam thing to do," complained Miss Geddes. "Taking a girl's harpoon away."

"Come on, Moby Dick," said George, lifting his wife to her feet. "Let's go home and spawn."

With many a laugh and cheer they made their exit. Now only Miss Geddes and I were left.

My hostess sat on the sofa, elbow on knee, chin in hand, pensive. "What a subject you would make for Rodin," I said with a warm smile.

She looked up. "You there," she said, "let's have some fun."

"What would you like to do, ma'am?" I asked politely.

"Think of something, stupid," she replied.

"There are a few windows still unbroken," I suggested.

"Balls," she replied.

"How about turning in some false alarms?" I suggested.

"Balls," she replied.

A proposal to play Musical Chairs elicited the same response, and so did a dozen other suggestions. "Always the same old crap," she said peevishly. "Can't you think of anything *new*?"

Then all at once a bursting, blinding thought flashed into my mind. I grew faint with hopefulness. And yet at the same moment I knew it could not be. It was madness—*madness*. But was it? It had happened before. Could it not happen again?

Back and forth I paced, torn with indecision. A hundred times I made up my mind to try it, and a hundred times I faltered. At length I stopped pacing. My mind was made up. Come what might, I had to try it.

Slowly I started walking across the room to Miss Geddes. A glass of fine spirits stood on a table in my path. I paused to pick it up and drink it. Then on I went until I was by her side.

"Miss Geddes," I said, and I could not hear my voice over the pounding of my heart, "have you ever been married?"

CHAPTER 8

"You'll be crazy about her, Mother," I said.

"She ain't movin' in with us," said Mother.

"Ivanhoe Gardens—end of the line," said the driver, and we got off the bus.

Dad looked with awe at the splendid homes all around us. "Which one of these joints does she work in?" he asked.

"She doesn't work in any of them," I chuckled.

"Works outdoors, huh?" said Mother. "Pickin' up paper and stuff like that."

"No, no," I said. "She *lives* here."

Mother whipped out her darning egg.

"Honest, Mother," I cried, leaping behind Dad. "She *does.*"

"You mean one of these swell broads married *you?*" asked Mother, eying me suspiciously.

"Yes," I said simply.

"Get the hell out of here," said Mother.

"It's the truth, Mother."

Mother thought for a moment. "How many months gone was she?" she asked.

"Mother!" I said reproachfully.

"Nothing to be ashamed of, Son," smiled Dad. "Your mother was in labor when we got married."

"Someday," said Mother to Dad, "I'm gonna take that big upper lip of yours and pull it over the top of your head like a cabbage leaf."

She said some more things too, but Dad lowered the ear-laps on his cap and spared himself.

We were in front of the Geddes house. "Here we are," I said. We crossed the moat and went up the mother-of-pearl path to the door. A lawn, smooth as a fairway, extended for a hundred feet on either side of the path. On one side of the lawn was a privet hedge, trimmed to spell out GEDDES. On the other side was a small circular pool over which leaned a bronze nymph from whose nipples came two ever-replenishing jets of water. Mother and Dad were silent—impressed, as I was, by the quiet good taste of everything.

Waving hello to a crew of glaziers replacing the windows broken in the previous night's revelry, I rang the doorbell.

After a short interval a distinguished-looking man with a white moustache and pince-nez opened the door. He looked at us askance.

"Are you Mr. Geddes?" I asked.

He nodded.

I clasped his hand warmly. "Dad," I breathed.

He wrenched his hand free in alarm. He stared hard at me, then at Dad, then at Mother. Recognition came into his eyes when he spied Mother. "Emma," he said, "what are you doing here?"

"Hiya," mumbled Mother.

"Then you know each other!" I exclaimed with delight.

"I used to scrub floors in his office," explained Mother.

"Well, well, well," I smiled.

Dad extended his hand. "I'm Oscar Riddle," he confessed. "I think dowries are a charming custom."

"What," demanded my father-in-law, "is going on here?"

"They're my folks, Dad Geddes," I explained with a chuckle.

Dad Geddes stamped his foot. "Who the hell are you?" he screamed.

"Harry," I smiled.

"What do you want?" he shouted.

"Fifteen thousand," said Dad. "For a start, I mean. Later we can expand."

Dad Geddes clenched his hands. "Look," he said slowly, "I'm very tired. I just got home from a trip. My daughter had a party last night and I found the house in a shambles."

"Little minx," I smiled.

Dad Geddes continued. "I've got a headache. I would like to lie down. Will you please state your business and leave?"

"Then Miss Geddes hasn't told you?" I asked.

"Told me what?"

"Naturally I expect to make you a partner," said Dad. "Junior partner, of course."

"Miss Geddes and I got married last night," I said with a blush.

"Winifred!" shrieked Dad Geddes. "Winifred! Winifred!"

A distinguished-looking lady with elegantly coifed gray hair came rushing out to the stoop. "What is it, Archer?" she asked, looking with grave concern at his deep purple face. "Who are these dreadful people?"

"Mother Geddes," I said tenderly and kissed her cheek.

She leaped with a scream upon her husband's back.

"The way I look at it," said Dad, "caps are due for a big comeback."

"One of these individuals claims he is married to Esme," said Dad Geddes.

"Give them some money and they'll go away," said Mother Geddes.

"Now you're talkin'," said Dad.

"I can't blame you for being surprised," I said. "It *was* rather sudden. But we'll make up for it. We'll all see a lot of each other."

They shuddered.

Mother strode over and seized Mother Geddes by her bodice. "Think you're better than I am, huh?" she asked.

"Please," said Mother Geddes.

"Tell you what," suggested Mother. "I'll wrestle you for a hundred bucks."

"Please," said Mother Geddes.

"A game of pool, then," said Mother. "I'll give you the fifteen ball and shoot left-handed."

Dad took Dad Geddes's arm. "While the ladies are talking woman-talk," he said, "why don't you and I go into the study and discuss our cap factory?"

"Perhaps," I suggested, with a look at the circle of curious glaziers who had gathered around us, "we had all better go inside."

"Yes," said my mother-in-law. She dismounted from my father-in-law and led the way into the living room.

"Now let's get to the bottom of this," said Dad Geddes. "Emma, will you kindly unhand my wife?"

Mother released her wristlock on Mother Geddes.

Dad Geddes turned to me. "Now, you claim you married my daughter last night?"

"A whirlwind courtship, you might call it," I smiled.

"The beauty part of a cap," said Dad, "is that it sits right against your head. You take a hat, it's got thirty-eight cubic inches of cold air between your scalp and the crown."

"What proof do you have of your marriage?" Dad Geddes asked me.

I handed him my marriage license with a warm smile.

"Flabby," said Mother, prodding Mother Geddes in the abdomen. "Your gut hangs like a peplum."

"Bully," said Mother Geddes.

Dad Geddes examined the marriage license. "It's a trick of some kind," he said.

"Oh no, sir," I protested. "Ask Miss Geddes."

"I intend to," he said. He walked to the foot of the stairs and called, "Esme! Esme, come down here at once."

"How much can you lift?" Mother asked Mother Geddes.

"I'm sure I don't know," replied Mother Geddes.

"Look," said Mother. She put her shoulder under the corner of the Steinway and raised it six feet off the ground.

"That's very impressive, no doubt," said Mother Geddes, "but we are seldom called upon to lift pianos in my set."

"Think how many ways you can use a cap," said Dad. He took his cap out of his pocket and put it on his head. "For ordinary weather," he said. He let down the earlaps. "For cold weather," he said. He tucked the earlaps back and turned the cap around with the vizor pointing backward. "For motoring," he said. He let down the earlaps. "For cold-weather motoring," he said.

Miss Geddes came down the stairs.

"Mother," I said, "put down the piano and come meet my wife."

Taking Mother and Dad by the hand, I advanced to greet Miss Geddes. If the test of married love is to love one's wife in the morning, I passed it beyond cavil on this forenoon. To put it bluntly, Miss Geddes looked awful. Her eyes were like two slots in a gum machine. Her complexion was the color of an apple that has been peeled and left in a warm room overnight. Her hair, which had been worn in an upsweep the night before, had now somehow become flattened on the top and looked like an irregular mortarboard. Her gait was eccentric, and her fingers jerked as though they were trying to leap off her hands.

But I loved her.

She stopped at the bottom of the stairs and clutched the newel post. "Miss Geddes," I said, "this is Mother and Dad Riddle."

"She don't look like she can lift much either," said Mother.

"I'm gonna put in a line of ladies' caps too," said Dad.

"Esme," said Dad Geddes, "nod once if you can understand me."

Her head rose and fell.

"Do you see these persons?"

She shook her head.

He pried one of her eyes open with his thumb and forefinger. "Now?"

She nodded.

"Did you marry the person in the middle last night?"

Miss Geddes fixed me with her open eye and looked for a long time. There was no sound except the crunch of Mother Geddes biting her knuckles. Miss Geddes's other eye opened independently for a moment and quickly closed again. A spasm of twitching passed over her frame. She nodded.

"We are undone!" cried Mother Geddes and flung herself to the floor.

"No, by George," thundered Dad Geddes. "We'll fight this thing. We'll have it annulled."

"You can't, Dad Geddes." I blushed hotly. "It's been consummated."

"You can't prove that!" he shouted.

"But I can. There were witnesses."

"Witnesses!" he gasped.

"Not many," I admitted. "Only a dozen or so. It was pretty late at night."

"But where——"

"On the courthouse steps," I giggled.

Miss Geddes's arms slid down the newel post and she joined her mother on the floor.

"My God!" croaked Dad Geddes, banging his fist into his forehead.

"What's so terrible?" shrugged Dad. "Look at it this way: you haven't lost a daughter; you've gained a son."

"Archer," said Mother Geddes to Dad Geddes, "we'll have to leave the country at once."

"Of course," he replied. "I'll make reservations for this afternoon."

"Don't forget to write," I smiled. "Even if it's only a postcard."

"Say," said Dad, "I bet you could use a few steamer caps."

Dad Geddes pulled his wife to her feet. "Let's go up and pack."

They started up the stairs. Mother Geddes stopped suddenly. "Where will you and Esme live?" she asked me.

I blushed hotly. "It's been consummated."

"Not with me," said Mother.

"I know of a room behind Schultz's bakery," I said. "Right next to the oven. Very warm in winter."

"Oh, Archer!" cried Mother Geddes, wringing her hands.

"All right," said Dad Geddes. "They can stay here. The house is theirs. My wedding present. Now let's get packed and get the hell out of here."

They went upstairs. Dad walked over to the sideboard and started filling his pockets with flat silver. Mother poked Miss Geddes's midriff with her toe.

"I give her two years," said Mother. "That's all. Then she'll be fatter'n the old lady."

CHAPTER 9

Mrs. Hargreaves opened the door of my office—Dad Geddes's office actually; I had taken it over when he left the country. It was a handsomely appointed office and suited me very well, although the constant clatter of stock tickers was rather annoying. Dad Geddes had been a broker during his residence in the United States.

Mrs. Hargreaves addressed me.

"What?" I shouted. I could not hear her over the din of the stock tickers.

She came close and yelled in my ear, "There's a guy here to see you."

"Now who would want to see me?" I bellowed.

"Damn if I know," she replied piercingly.

"All right. Show him in." I took her arm as she started to leave. "Mrs. Hargreaves," I roared, "you've worked here for a long time. Do you know how to turn off these tickers?"

She shook her head.

"And all this ticker tape that's piling up." I pointed to a great mass of paper writhing on the floor. "What should I do with it?"

She shrugged.

"Well, no matter," I shrieked. "Perhaps a parade will go by someday and I can throw it out the window. Show the gentleman in."

Mrs. Hargreaves undulated from my office. A most attractive woman, she. Extravagantly developed. But that, of course, was none of my concern. I was interested only in her clerical ability, although, to be sure, I had not yet had occasion to observe it. The fault was mine. She asked me every morning whether I had any letters to give her. Even if the noise of the tickers would have permitted dictation, I could think of nobody I wanted to write to, so I always had to decline Mrs. Hargreaves's offer with thanks. Lately I had been letting her take afternoons off. In fact, I took them off myself. Every afternoon I would black my face with burnt cork, go down to the Union Depot and carry bags until I had accumulated fifty cents, and then go to the movies.

Mrs. Hargreaves brought in a shark-toothed gentleman in a sharkskin suit. Because of the difficulty of hearing in my office, I had been practicing reading lips, and I watched the gentleman's mouth very carefully as he spoke to me. "My sow has a new Chevrolet," I thought he said.

Certain that that could not be correct, I shouted, "I beg your pardon?"

"I'm Payson Atterbury," he yelled.

"So much noise," I thundered apologetically. "Do you know how to turn these things off?"

He walked over to the tickers and did something I didn't quite see. The tickers fell silent.

"Thank you," I said gratefully. "Payson Atterbury? Not 'The Great Forecloser'?"

"The same," he confessed shyly.

I wrung his hand. "Well, I *am* glad to meet you, Mr. Atterbury. I've heard some fine things about your usurious practices."

"I had a lot of luck," he murmured. "But let's not talk about me. It's you I'm interested in. I'm a great friend of Esme's, and when I learned she was married, I had to drop in and say hello to her husband."

"That's right neighborly," I said.

"How are you and Esme getting along?"

"It's hard to tell," I admitted. "She hasn't spoken to me since our marriage."

"Busy, no doubt," said Mr. Atterbury.

"Perhaps," I replied doubtfully. "But I don't know what she can be doing. She just lies in bed all day with her face against the wall."

"Quite normal," Mr. Atterbury assured me.

I was much relieved.

"But enough of marital bliss," said Mr. Atterbury. "Let's get down to business. I'm a man of few words, Mr. Riddle."

"Maybe a thesaurus would help," I suggested.

"I have taken the liberty of investigating you, and I am very much impressed with your record as an attorney."

"You're funning me," I said.

"No," he insisted. "I know that things haven't gone well for you, but it's not your fault. You're just not a courtroom lawyer. Your legal talents lie in another direction—research, organization, planning."

This, indeed, was a facet of my personality I had not even suspected. I could not help but admire Mr. Atterbury for having discovered it.

"I could use a man like you," he said.

"Whatever for?" I asked.

"I pride myself on my ability to judge character, Mr. Riddle. I'm convinced that you are a man of intelligence, discretion, and loyalty. I have a top-secret job, and I have decided that you are the man I can trust with it."

I rose from my chair. "My hand, sir," I said.

"So it is," agreed Mr. Atterbury, examining it briefly.

"All right," I said briskly. "What must I do first?"

"First," he answered, "I want you to copy everything in Webster's New International Dictionary."

"Now isn't that a coincidence?" I chuckled. "I remember reading a Sherlock Holmes story where a man hired people to copy the Encyclopaedia Brittanica. He turned out to be a big crook."

"But I'm not hiring you to copy the Encyclopaedia Brittanica. I'm hiring you to copy Webster's New International Dictionary," Mr. Atterbury pointed out. "Therefore I can't be a crook."

"Obviously," I said.

"When you finish the dictionary, go out and count all the blocks in the city."

"Right, P.A.," I snapped.

"Take your time, do a good job, and, most important, remember this: The job is top secret. Don't let anybody know I retained you."

"Check, P.A."

"I'll be in touch with you. Good-by."

"Good-by, P.A."

He stopped as he was halfway out. "Oh, by the way, it's true that you're an old friend of George Overmeyer's, isn't it?"

"Right, P.A."

"Fine fellow, George. I hope you'll be seeing a lot of him."

"I hope so, P.A. I'll tell him you send your regards."

"No, no. No, no. Don't mention my name to George— or to anyone else, of course. Nobody must know about our connection. Top secret, remember?"

"Check, P.A."

"Well, good-by." He started out again, and again he paused. "I suppose you want your tickers turned back on," he said.

Before I could protest, he had somehow started them going again and was out the door.

I did not work that day. I spent several hours trying

to locate the shutoff switch, but all I accomplished was to catch my hand in the mechanism and get an order to sell 500 shares of Commonwealth and Southern at 34½ stamped on my palm where it is to this day.

CHAPTER 10

I got home about five-thirty that evening, kissed the maid, and tiptoed upstairs to see how Miss Geddes was feeling. As I came into her room she was sitting on a chaise longue talking to a tall, thin young woman dressed in the height of fashion. They did not notice my entrance.

"But what can I do, Mavis?" Miss Geddes was saying.

Now I recognized my wife's visitor: Mavis Atterbury, wife of Payson Atterbury and undisputed social leader of Ivanhoe Gardens. What a charming coincidence, I thought, to have Mr. Atterbury call on me and Mrs. Atterbury call on my wife all in the same day.

"You've got to try to make a go of this marriage, Esme," said Mrs. Atterbury.

"Have you seen him?" asked Miss Geddes.

Well, looks aren't everything, I thought.

"Well, looks aren't everything," said Mrs. Atterbury.

I nodded.

"He's lonesome," said Miss Geddes.

Perhaps she said "loathsome." I didn't quite catch it. My ears were still ringing from the noise of the stock tickers.

"You'll get used to it," said Mrs. Atterbury.

It must have been "loathsome."

"Many unattractive people learn to turn their handicaps to social assets," said Mrs. Atterbury. "Do you remember Emily Heath who went to Bennington with us?"

"The one who was drum majorette of the school band?"

"That's the one. Remember the time she threw her baton up in the air and lost it in the sun and it fell right through the top of her head?"

"Yes. And the doctors couldn't get it out."

"That's right. She had to go around with ten inches of chromium rod sticking out of her skull."

"Yes, I remember. She was pretty embarrassed about it. Left school finally, didn't she?"

"She went back home. At first she used to sit all day in a dark room and brood and refuse to see people."

Understandable, I thought.

"But after awhile," Mrs. Atterbury continued, "she got to thinking. She took some ribbons and flowers and tulle and tied them to the baton and went out. Everybody thought it was a hat and told her how chic it was. She began to change the decorations on her baton every time she went out, and pretty soon the whole town was raving about her hats. Last month she had an article in *Vogue* called 'How I Triumphed Over a Horrible Disfigurement to Become the Millinery Style Leader of Spokane, Washington.' "

"Maybe I ought to stick something in Harry's head," mused Miss Geddes.

I blanched.

"Oh, I don't think that's necessary," said Mrs. Atterbury.

My color returned.

"The thing to do," she went on, "is to find some characteristic of his that can be used to make him socially acceptable."

"Like what?" asked Miss Geddes.

"I haven't met your husband. What would you say is his outstanding trait?"

"He's real dumb," replied Miss Geddes promptly.

"That has never been a disadvantage in society," observed Mrs. Atterbury. "Tell me some more about him."

"He's ungainly, crude, gauche——"

"There you have it!" cried Mrs. Atterbury. "A rough diamond. How refreshing it will be to have a passionate, brooding man in our set."

I knit my brows and brooded passionately.

"Naah," said Miss Geddes. "He's a little pip-squeak—a toady. He fawns all over everybody."

"Even more interesting," said Mrs. Atterbury. "A smooth rough-diamond."

"Look, Mavis, it's hopeless. I'm going to Reno tomorrow and get this thing over with."

I almost cried out, so distressed was I. I suddenly saw

all my recent gains slipping away—this fine house, my splendid office, albeit noisy, Dad Geddes's suits. And, of course, also my wife, with whom I was enchanted. Distance lends enchantment.

"You mustn't do it, Esme," said Mrs. Atterbury. "Divorce is so ugly."

"*You've* had three," Miss Geddes pointed out.

"All ugly," said Mrs. Atterbury. "I'll never have three divorces again."

"No, Mavis——"

"Give it a whirl, Esme. Speak to him, take him to parties, try to make him a part of your life."

"You're not suggesting that I extend him a husband's privileges?"

I leaned forward eagerly.

"Of course not. No need to overdo it."

I shrugged philosophically. I could always take up squash racquets.

"Try it for a little while," urged Mrs. Atterbury. "Six months. If it doesn't work out, you can get a Florida divorce. It will be winter by then."

"Why are you so interested?" asked Miss Geddes.

"Because I'm terribly fond of you," replied Mrs. Atterbury.

There was no doubting her sincerity, the crossed fingers behind her back notwithstanding.

Miss Geddes pondered for a moment. "I was going down to Florida anyhow next January," she said thoughtfully. "There's some alligators down there making a bag for me."

"Then why not wait until then to get your divorce?"

"All right. I'll give it a try."

"That's my good girl. Now I must rush."

I stole from the room and ran downstairs, cheering softly, to tell the good news to the maid.

CHAPTER 11

On every second Wednesday during the summer Wrose Wrigley, poetess laureate of Ivanhoe Gardens, held intimate alfresco suppers, during which she favored her guests with recitations of her verse and prose. Naturally only the most cultured were invited to these gatherings; one had either to belong to the Book-of-the-Month Club or to know somebody who did.

I had long yearned to attend a Wrose Wrigley party, but never in my wildest dreams did I imagine that I would ever be invited. (My wildest dreams, incidentally, are pretty wild. The other night, for example, I dreamt I was attending a polo match aboard the *Queen Mary*. All the spectators except me had pencil sharpeners with which they were putting points on frankfurters. So distressed was I at not having a pencil sharpener that I burst into tears, whereupon a nude young woman tapped me on the shoulder and informed me that I had just been elected lieutenant governor of Vermont. At this intelligence I became very excited and climbed the young woman, who had now

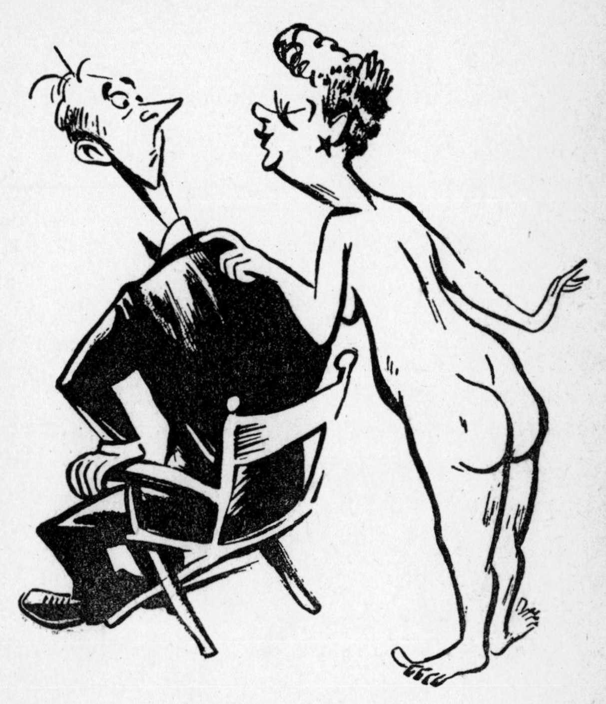

"You've just been elected lieutenant governor of Vermont."

turned into a ladder. Then I woke. . . . George Overmeyer, a keen student of Freud, to whom I later described this dream, said that its meaning was quite obvious: I had an unfulfilled desire to visit Yellowstone Park.)

But I digress. I was telling how come I got invited to a Wrose Wrigley party. It happened shortly after Mavis Atterbury left my wife's bedroom. I was eating my dinner when Miss Geddes entered the kitchen. I sprang instantly to my feet. "You there," said Miss Geddes. "I want to talk to you."

"And I to you," I declared fervently, "for conversation is the currency of marriage. Only by speaking freely can the little irritations be dispelled that are so natural to matrimony. I had looked upon our union," I confessed, "as a long conversation piece, the two of us growing older, but the talk ever flowing until, at length, we are laid to rest in a common sepulcher."

Miss Geddes swore a mighty oath and poured herself a tumbler of cooking sherry. "Listen," she said. "Against my better judgment, I've decided to give this marriage a try until winter . . . Stop jumping up and down! From now on you can take your meals with me in the dining room. You'll escort me when we go out and act as host when we entertain at home . . . Will you stop?"

Jumping up and down, she meant.

"As far as our friends are concerned, we will behave as husband and wife. However, we will continue to have separate bedrooms."

I stopped jumping up and down.

"Now go on upstairs and get dressed. We're going over to Wrose Wrigley's."

So casually did she mention the name that its full import did not dawn on me until I was upstairs dressing. Wrose

Wrigley! I became so agitated that I had to ring for the maid to button me.

But even with the maid's assistance my habit was not all it should have been. This I learned when I joined Miss Geddes in the living room. "You don't wear a turtle-neck sweater with a tuxedo!" she exclaimed sharply. "Kee-rist," she added and poured herself a hooker of brandy.

In a trice my slight error was rectified and Miss Geddes and I were driving merrily to Wrose Wrigley's house. I was possibly more merry than she.

We reached the Wrigley house, drove over the moat, and parked in the jousting ground. From the courtyard we could hear the sounds of well-bred revelry. How the *mots justes* must be crackling, I thought, how delicious must be the badinage—a thrust here, a parry there, an endless contest of wit and literacy, endlessly delightful. I gave a little shiver.

No less a personage than Wrose Wrigley herself greeted us at the courtyard gate. How shall I describe my hostess? Where to begin? Her eyes, perhaps, were her most arresting feature. Minute and milky, they seemed at first glance like a pair of ball bearings; in moments of passion, as I was to discover later, they rolled back into her head and quite disappeared. Her nose was piquantly kiltered. An inscrutable smile played over her dentures. Moles and related tumescences gave her face an attractive irregularity.

Her body can best be described as womanly. A peekaboo blouse revealed a full, checkered bosom (the result, I learned later, of sun-bathing behind a lattice). A multicolored dirndl strained at her commodious hips. Her conical legs ended in the smallest adult feet in the Occident.

It was difficult to guess her age, so I asked her. She replied with a tap of her fan that broke the skin on my forehead. Chuckling rather more than my wife, I followed Miss Wrigley into the garden where the guests were seated.

Many of the guests were people I had met at that memorable party at Miss Geddes's house, but although the cast of characters, so to speak, was largely the same as had graced Miss Geddes's party, the nature of tonight's gathering was entirely different. Where Miss Geddes's party had frankly been a vehicle for relaxation, this soiree, while no less pleasurable, had behind it a more serious purpose—to promote the arts, to instruct, to edify, to discuss, to shed light on those aspects of American culture that touched the lives of all us members of the middle class.

I was a listener, rather than a participant, in most of the conversation that evening. When I got home I put down as much as I could remember in my diary (Dad Geddes's diary, actually). Let me quote an excerpt from my diary, a typical sample of the kind of talk that went on at Wrose Wrigley's party:

MR. OXNARD: I read a mighty interesting book last night.

MRS. HOLLOWAY: I just never get time to read any more, what with——

MR. HERWIG (interrupting): What was the name of the book?

MRS. HOLLOWAY: Name of the book? Lord, I just never get time to read any more.

MR. HERWIG: I meant the book Ed (Mr. Oxnard) was reading.

MRS. HOLLOWAY: Oh.

MR. OXNARD: I forget exactly. Mae (Mrs. Oxnard) would know. Mae?

MR. SUNDBERG: She went to the john.

MR. OXNARD: Well, when she comes back she'll know. (NOTE: *As it turned out, Mrs. Oxnard never did come back.*)

MR. ATTERBURY: I understand there's a lot of money in the book game.

MR. BENSON: The movie game, that's where the money is. Why, I hear Gregory Peck spends fifty thousand dollars a year on milk baths alone.

MR. BRADBURY: I've got a cousin in the weather-stripping game out in California, he tells me Ingrid Bergman is bald as an egg.

MRS. McEWEN: It's those milk baths. They clog your follicles.

MR. WHITE: Speaking of follicles, Leopold Stokowski is coming to the auditorium next Friday.

MR. KRAFT: I hear he's got a cork leg.

MR. ATTERBURY: I understand there's a lot of money in the cork-leg game.

And so it went all evening long, I sitting there listening avidly and regretting that I had never learned shortarm so

I could take it all down verbatim. I put down as much as I could recall when I arrived home, but I'm sure I forgot many an exchange equally as meaty as the one quoted above.

At midnight Miss Wrigley cried cheerily, "Soup's on!" a colorful term denoting that supper was served. The guests flocked to a gaily festooned table on which peanut-butter sandwiches were arranged to spell out: *ARS LONGA, VITA BREVIS.* "What the hell does that mean?" said several, feigning ignorance of this classic Greek phrase. With many a laugh and cheer, the tasty repast was dispatched.

Supper over, Miss Wrigley lighted candles and announced with a blush that she would now read her latest work. "Good heavens, look what time it's getting to be!" cried everyone, glancing at his watch. Hastily they made their good-bys and departed.

Thus it became my privilege to be the sole member of the audience at the first reading of Wrose Wrigley's latest work.

"Dear me, this always happens," said Miss Wrigley, watching the last of the guests leaping over the hedge. "Well, no matter," she smiled. "I'll read to you, Mr. Riddle."

"Sweet," I murmured.

"It's a poem," she said, "called *My Garden.*"

"Sweet," I murmured.

She read in her ringing baritone:

"My garden it is fragrant,
The blossoms they do bloom,
So wild and free and flagrant
Out of the earth's sweet womb.

"When you pass it, neighbor,
And see the flowers grow
Do you realize the labor
It took to make it so?

"The hoeing and the weeding,
The spraying and the work,
For the art of flower breeding,
It never lets you shirk.

"A gardener is wiser
The moment that he knows
It takes a heap of fertilizer
To make a rose a rose."

"Jolly!" I cried. "Capital!"

"I write prose too," she confessed. "Stories, essays, mottoes."

And now I had a confession to make. "I'd give anything to be able to write," I said, rubbing my toe in the turf.

"But you can!" she exclaimed. "I'm sure you can."

I smiled bravely. "No. I've tried a million times. I just never know how to start. I think if I could get past the beginning, the rest would come easily."

"I know, I know. Beginnings used to be difficult for me,

too, until I learned the secret." She slipped her hand inside my shirt and tapped my chest to emphasize her words. "The beginning of a story must excite the interest of the reader, must make him eager to know what is coming."

"Ah," I said, comprehending. "You mean the beginning of a story must be arresting and startling."

"Exactly."

"Now let me see if I can think of one." I knit my brows in thought. Miss Wrigley gripped my upper thighs to help me concentrate. Suddenly a perfect beginning occurred to me. I leaped up excitedly, upsetting Miss Wrigley upon the lawn. I brushed her off—twice, at her insistence.

"I've got it, Miss Wrigley," I shouted. "I've got the perfect beginning. Listen . . . 'Bang! Bang! Bang! Bang! Four shots ripped into my groin and I was off on the biggest adventure of my life.' "

"Splendid," said my hostess. "It's got everything."

I glowed with pleasure. Now, if I ever wrote a book, I would know how to begin it.

Gratefully I took Miss Wrigley's hands in mine. "How will I ever thank you for what you taught me tonight?"

She drew me down beside her on the glider. "I can teach you a lot more," she whispered.

Suddenly—I could scarcely believe it—her lips were on mine and she was wrenching at my clothing.

I tore myself away. "You're mad!" I cried hoarsely.

"Yes. Yes. Mad for you." She resumed her advances.

"Miss Wrigley," I said coldly, "please desist. I'm just not that kind of a boy."

"Nonsense. You're a normal human being with normal impulses. Why deny them?"

"May I remind you that I am a married man?"

"But what has that to do with us?"

"Why, everything!"

"I know what you're going to say about fidelity and all that outmoded rot."

"Outmoded rot! Why, it's the very foundation stone of marriage."

"Silly boy! Have I suggested that you leave your wife?"

"No, but——"

"Have I proposed any long-term arrangement between us?"

"No, but——"

"All I ask is that the two of us while away an idle hour with a very natural and pleasant act."

"It's more than that. To me it's one of the most beautiful and important things in the world."

"Who's arguing?"

"Well, then——"

"Look. Do you know what repressions are?"

"Sure. That's when everybody's out of work."

"No, no. *Re*pressions."

"Oh. . . . No."

"That's when you stifle a natural instinct. Very bad for you. Makes you nauseous."

"Maybe so, but I can't do it. I can't do anything that I can't tell my wife about. I don't think married people should have secrets."

"Ridiculous. Nobody tells his wife everything. There are certain things you do in private, like clipping the hairs in your nostrils."

"How did you know?"

"Let's get going!"

"So, you see, you really have no argument. Let's get going."

"But I don't love you."

"This has nothing to do with love. This is pure friendship. You are a fine, sensitive person, the kind I want for a friend, to be close to. And nothing brings people closer together than the act I propose."

"It does that," I had to admit.

"This above all, Mr. Riddle, to thine own self be true. Be true to the natural, normal instincts that are your strength, your very life—not to the bigotry and superstition and *sickness* that others would impose on you. That's your choice here: between sickness and health, between progress and reaction, between light and darkness. Which will you choose?"

I made a choice that all who prefer health to sickness, progress to reaction, and light to darkness would have to applaud.

CHAPTER 12

I sat in my office the following afternoon spinning in my swivel chair and thinking about Wrose Wrigley's party and all the things I had learned about literature and repressions and outmoded morality. A man had come that morning and removed Dad Geddes's stock tickers, so I was happily able to pursue my thoughts in quiet.

There was a knock on my door and my secretary, Mrs. Hargreaves, entered. "Mr. Atterbury to see you," she announced.

"Show him in," I cried cordially and gave him a warm handshake as he entered. "Splendid party last night, what?" I said.

"Fine," he agreed. "I was glad to see you didn't say anything to anybody about my retaining you."

"Mums the word, P.A."

"Good boy. And remember, if anybody asks if you're working for me, the answer is no."

"Roger," I snapped.

"How you getting along with George Overmeyer?"

"Oh, famously."

"Good. Fine fellow, George. Well, I'll be seeing you." He started to leave.

"Sir," I called, "wouldn't you like to look over the work I've been doing for you? I've got Webster's New International Dictionary copied halfway through the E's." I pointed at a stack of papers on my desk.

"That's fine, boy. Keep up the good work. I'll look at it some other time." He left.

What a yummy man, I thought. How fortunate that I should have found such a good client. On the other hand, how fortunate for him to have found a lawyer who would do such a bang-up job of copying the dictionary. Fortunate, both of us.

I rang for Mrs. Hargreaves and she came in with her notebook. "Where did we leave off this morning?" I asked.

She consulted her notes. "Erotetic," she replied.

I pulled the dictionary toward me. Mrs. Hargreaves settled herself on the leather divan, crossed her knees, and poised her pencil over her notebook. I found my place in the dictionary and began dictating. "'Erotic (ē·rŏt′ĭk) *adj.* [Gr. *erōtikos.* See Eros.] 1. Of, pertaining to, or treating of, sexual love; amatory. 2. Strongly affected by sexual desire . . .'"

And strongly affected I was this minute as I looked at

Mrs. Hargreaves on the divan. Her sheer summer dress clung enviably to her abundant curves; the pretty pink tip of her tongue kept darting out of the side of her mouth as she concentrated on her Gregg. I glanced at her speculatively for a while. At length, "Why not?" I said to myself and rose from my desk. I walked over to her side.

She looked up. "Yes?" she said.

In lieu of reply I seized her in my arms and rained kisses on her bee-stung lips.

She tore herself away. "You're mad!" she cried hoarsely.

"Yes. Yes. Mad for you." I resumed my advances.

"Mr. Riddle," she said coldly, "please desist. I'm just not that kind of a girl."

"Nonsense. You're a normal human being with normal impulses. Why deny them?"

"May I remind you that I am a married woman?"

"But what has that to do with us?"

"Why, everything!"

"I know what you're going to say about fidelity and all that outmoded rot."

"Outmoded rot! Why, it's the very foundation stone of marriage."

"Silly girl! Have I suggested that you leave your husband?"

"No, but—"

"Have I proposed any long-term arrangement between us?"

"No, but—"

"All I ask is that the two of us while away an idle hour with a very natural and pleasant act."

"It's more than that. To me it's one of the most beautiful and important things in the world."

"Who's arguing?"

"Well, then——"

"Look. Do you know what repressions are?"

"Sure. That's when everybody's out of work."

"No, no. *Re*pressions."

"Oh. . . . No."

"That's when you stifle a natural instinct. Very bad for you. Makes you nauseous."

"Maybe so, but I can't do it. I can't do anything that I can't tell my husband about. I don't think married people should have secrets."

"Ridiculous. Nobody tells her husband everything. There are certain things you do in private, like clipping the hairs in your nostrils."

"How did you know?"

"So, you see, you really have no argument. Let's get going."

"But I don't love you."

"This has nothing to do with love. This is pure friendship. You are a fine, sensitive person, the kind I want for a friend, to be close to. And nothing brings people closer together than the act I propose."

"It does that," she had to admit.

"This above all, Mrs. Hargreaves, to thine own self be true. Be true to the natural, normal instincts that are your strength, your very life—not to the bigotry and superstition and *sickness* that others would impose on you. That's your choice here: between sickness and health, between progress and reaction, between light and darkness. Which will you choose?"

Confidently I closed in on her.

She pushed me away. "But what if I get pregnant?" she said.

"Hmm," I said. This had not come up last night. "Excuse me," I said.

I went to the phone and dialed Wrose Wrigley for instructions, but her maid said she was out buying hormones. There was nothing for me to do but ad-lib it.

I returned to Mrs. Hargreaves. "What was your last statement again?" I asked.

"I said what if I get pregnant."

"Oh. . . . Well, that's better than being repressed."

That sounded a little lame.

"And it's too hot," said Mrs. Hargreaves.

"Heat's nothing but a repression," I said.

That didn't sound so good either.

"Look," she said, "if you feel this way, why don't you go home to your wife?"

"That's all you know about it," I replied with a sad smile. Sighing, I got to my feet. "Well, we might as well go back to work."

We got all the way through the H's that afternoon.

CHAPTER 13

Shortly after noon on a September Saturday, George Overmeyer dropped in and said, "What are you kids doing?"

"Nothing much," I said truthfully. I was leafing through my high-school annual. Miss Geddes was sticking pins in a wax image of me.

"Come on over for lunch," said George.

"But aren't you going to the races this afternoon?" I asked.

"The track closed last week," he answered. "I'll have to lose my money on out-of-town races until next spring."

"How's Agnes?" Miss Geddes inquired politely. "Too drunk to talk?"

"She just got up," said George. "She'll be articulate for two, three more hours."

So we got into George's car and drove over to his house, first stopping at his liquor store where he picked up several cases of whisky and took all the money out of the cash register. His store was a large, well-patronized establishment situated just outside Ivanhoe Gardens. There were no other liquor stores in the vicinity; George's late father-in-law, who had taken an active interest in civic affairs, had succeeded in persuading the Board of Aldermen not to grant any more liquor licenses in the area after he got his.

It was a warm afternoon and the pitcher of cold martini cocktails that awaited us at George's house was more than welcome. A delicious light lunch was served—cantaloupe halves filled with bourbon—and then we repaired to the terrace for brandy.

The conversation started lazily. "I hear," said Mrs. Overmeyer, "that Ethel had her ovaries cut out."

"Green?" said Miss Geddes.

"Yes," said Mrs. Overmeyer.

"It's just as well," I said. "Green ovaries can be mighty dangerous."

"Schmuck," said Miss Geddes. "The woman's name is Green."

"Oh," I said.

"I kind of envy Ethel," said Mrs. Overmeyer. "One thing is sure: she won't be having any goddam kids."

"Surely you can't mean that," I protested. "Children are the most wonderful thing in the world. I'd love to have one—or at least the chance to try for one."

"No, Schmuck," said Mrs. Overmeyer to me, "you're better off without 'em. I know. I've got one, and she's nothing but trouble."

"But how can she be?" I asked. "You've got a fine big house and yard, a nurse to take care of her—"

"That's not the point," replied Mrs. Overmeyer. "Did you see *The Snake Pit?*"

"Yes."

"*Lady in the Dark? Spellbound?* All those other psychological things?"

"Yes."

"In every single one of those pictures, people go nuts because of something their parents did to them when they were kids."

"But what has that to do with you?" I asked. "You and George would never treat a child unkindly or cruelly."

"You don't get the idea at all," answered Mrs. Overmeyer. "In those movies the parents weren't unkind or cruel. They were perfect bricks to their children. And yet they did some mild little thing—something so unimportant they didn't even notice it—and twenty years later the kids end up in the laughing academy. Remember *Lady in the Dark?* Remember what knocked the heroine off her trolley? When she was a little girl, her mother was all dressed up to go to a party. The girl wanted to kiss the mother good night, but the mother wouldn't let her because she was afraid the girl would muss her hair. The next thing you know, the girl's got a neurosis as big as the Ritz."

Mrs. Overmeyer poured herself another brandy and continued. "Who knows what goes on in their goddam subconsciouses? *Anything* can be traumatic, and it's always the parents' fault. It doesn't matter what you do for a kid—

you buy him toys and candy and clothes; you send him to camps, take him to shows, bring him on trips; you never say a hard word to him—and then one day you happen accidently to scowl at him and—wham!—he thinks he's Napoleon."

She sighed mightily. "How do you cope with something like that? Take our daughter Linda—a mean little bastard if you ever saw one. A good clout in the chops is what she needs. But how can we risk it? We're scared even to raise our voices to her. How do we know what would happen? We yell at her today and ten years later she's exposing herself on streetcars."

"Ahem, ahem," said George loudly, casting a meaningful glance in the direction of the doorway.

We turned and there stood Linda herself, accompanied by a heavily bandaged nurse. She was a beautiful child, fair, blond, and blue-eyed.

"Linda! Linda darling!" cried Mrs. Overmeyer. "Come in and say hello to everybody. You know Esme—and this is her husband, Mr. Riddle."

"How do you do, little lady?" I said with a warm smile.

"You're ugly and I hate you," replied Linda. "I would like to tear your skin off in big, ragged patches."

"Perhaps you can some afternoon, dear," said Mrs. Overmeyer.

"I don't know," I said quickly. "I'm pretty busy."

"Come here to Mommy, sweetheart," said Mrs. Overmeyer. "Would you like to muss Mommy's hair?"

"Shut your big dumb mouth," said Linda.

"All right, dear," said Mrs. Overmeyer. "But you be sure to let Mommy know whenever you want to muss her hair. Mommy loves you very much, and so does Daddy. Don't you, Daddy?"

"I found some dollars on your dresser and . . ."

"Passionately," said George. "Come over here, little succubus, and tell Daddy what you've been doing all afternoon."

"I've been up in your bedroom," said Linda. "I found some dollars on your dresser and I flushed them down the toilet."

"Agnes," said George, "listen to me. *The Snake Pit, Lady*

in the Dark, all those others—they were just movies. What makes you so sure they're accurate?"

"They had technical advisers," replied his wife. "Now, George, you know what to say."

"All right," mumbled George. He patted Linda on the head. "I cannot find words to describe my exultation at learning that you have flushed all my dollars down the toilet," he said. "Tomorrow, unfortunately, is Sunday, so I am unable to go to the store and get any more dollars for you to flush. However, I do have some negotiable securities in the house, and those are at your disposal."

"See how much Daddy loves you?" said Mrs. Overmeyer. "And so does Mommy. Are you quite sure you wouldn't like to muss Mommy's hair before you go up for your nap?"

"I want to hear a story before I go to sleep," said Linda, "or else I'll burn the house down."

"Of course, dear," replied her mother. "Miss Wilkins will tell you one. Won't you, Miss Wilkins?"

The nurse shook her head dumbly. Her face was taped right up to the eyes.

"I hit her with an educational toy," giggled Linda.

"Well, then Daddy will tell you a story."

Linda pointed at me. "I want him to come too. I want to pinch him while I'm listening."

Not wishing to contribute to any possible trauma, I agreed. Up to the nursery we went, and while the child raised welts on my midriff, George told the following story:

Once upon a time there was a little creep who lived in a mailbox. One night while he was fast asleep, a truck from the post office drove up. The driver got out, opened the mailbox, dumped the contents in a sack, and threw the sack into the truck. This happened so fast that the little creep didn't have time to cry out. Before he could open his mouth, the truck was moving. "Let me out! Let me out!" cried the little creep. But the truck was making so much noise—*brrrm, brrrm, brrrm, brrrm*—that nobody could hear the little creep.

In a little while the truck stopped. The sack was taken out and thrown into an airplane. This happened so fast that the little creep didn't have time to cry out. Before he could open his mouth, the airplane was flying. "Let me out! Let me out!" cried the little creep. But the airplane was making so much noise—*rrrrouwho, rrrrouwho, rrrrouwho, rrrrouwho*—that nobody could hear the little creep.

By and by the airplane landed. The sack was taken out and thrown into another truck. This happened so fast that the little creep didn't have time to cry out. Before he could open his mouth, the truck was moving. "Let me out! Let me out!" cried the little creep. But the truck was making so much noise—*brrrm, brrrm, brrrm, brrrm*—that nobody could hear the little creep.

Pretty soon the truck stopped. The sack was taken out and thrown into a train. This happened so fast that the little creep didn't have time to cry out. Before he could open his mouth, the train was moving. "Let me out! Let me out!" cried the little creep. But the train was making so much noise—*clickety-clack, clickety-clack, clickety-clack, clickety-clack*—that nobody could hear the little creep.

After a while the train stopped. The sack was taken out and

thrown into another truck. This happened so fast that the little creep didn't have time to cry out. Before he could open his mouth the truck was moving. "Let me out! Let me out!" cried the little creep. But the truck was making so much noise—*brrrm, brrrm, brrrm, brrrm*—that nobody could hear the little creep.

Presently the truck stopped. It stopped in front of a post office. The sack was carried inside. The postmaster opened the sack and shook it out on the counter. Then he saw the little creep.

"Well, what have we here?" said the postmaster.

"Please, sir," said the creep, "I'm a creep."

The postmaster held the creep up and looked at him very closely. "Hmm," he said. "No postage, no address, no return address. I will send you to the dead-letter office."

"But, sir," said the creep, "I'm not a letter. I'm a creep."

The postmaster took out a revolver and shot the creep right between the eyes.

"In that case," said the postmaster, "I will send you to the dead-creep office."

George and I left Linda sitting upright and blinking rapidly. "If I can't belt her," said George, "I can at least confuse her."

CHAPTER 14

I knocked lightly on the door. "Miss Geddes," I called. "Miss Geddes."

"What do you want?" she inquired from within her bedroom.

"I thought you might like something before you retired. . . . I know *I* would."

"Get the hell out of here," said my wife.

With a brave little smile, I turned and went downstairs. Three months married, and, except for the first night, still an unkissed groom. In fact, I remembered ruefully, there had been no kissing on the first night either. The other, yes; kissing, no.

Suddenly depressed, I went into the kitchen to fix myself a snack. When I am low in my mind, nothing cheers me up like food. I poured a jar of anchovies over a beef tongue and fell to. As always, food helped. By the time I finished the beef tongue, my heart had stopped aching. After eating a bottle of maraschino cherries and a tin of pork shoulder, my melancholy was quite dissipated.

I opened a can of pearl onions and reflected calmly. I took, you might say, an inventory. What had I had three months ago? What did I have today?

The first advantage was staring me in the face. Through the open door of the refrigerator I could see bottles of milk and cream, slabs of cheese, platters of meat, cans of beer, condiments and relishes, appetizers, vegetables, desserts, juices, fruits, preserves. And what had there been in my father's refrigerator? I'll tell you what: caps.

Take clothes. Three months ago I had owned a single suit, a factory reject. Today the abundant wardrobe of Dad Geddes was all mine. I had suits for every conceivable occasion—lounge suits, business suits, sports suits, formal suits, even a Tyrolean suit with short leather britches. (For a while I thought I'd never have occasion to wear the Tyrolean outfit, but I finally did get a chance. The Civic Opera Company put on *William Tell,* and I wore it to the performance.)

Today I had a waterproof room. Today I had money in my pocket. Today I had a cigarette lighter with a pencil on the other end. Had any of these conditions obtained three months ago? They had not.

And consider my professional status. For the first time I was a busy and successful attorney. Of all the lawyers in town, Payson Atterbury had chosen me to copy Webster's

New International Dictionary and count all the blocks in the city. It was a massive undertaking, and I could not but feel proud that Mr. Atterbury had considered my legal talents sufficient for the task.

I opened a can of pie cherries. In three short months tremendous gains had accrued to me. The credit side of my ledger was loaded. On the debit side, there was only one entry: my wife denied me her bed.

I do not mean to minimize this fact. Make no mistake: it troubled me, some nights acutely. On one such night I conceived a desperate plan. Putting on false whiskers and disguising my voice, I knocked on my wife's door and told her I had come to read her meter. Unfortunately, my ruse was doomed to failure; the real meter reader was already in bed with her.

Unarguably my love life was unsatisfactory. But, I asked myself as I munched a cold ear of corn, was that much of a price to pay for what I had gained? It was not. Never had one man got so much for so little. Besides, I could always call on Wrose Wrigley. Or, better still, take cold showers.

And anyhow, who knew what might happen? Miss Geddes might suddenly change toward me. Living under the same roof as we were, she could not continue to ignore my not inconsiderable charms. Admittedly I still had some rough edges, but they were daily fewer. I was steadily becoming more poised, more suave, more full of graces. Surely my wife would have to notice it.

And I would cultivate additional talents that were certain to please her. I would take up the mandolin. I would learn the maxixe. I would memorize Kipling's *If*. I would buy a gold-headed walking stick. The woman was only flesh and blood; could she resist all this?

Where there's a will, I told myself, opening a jar of Maatjes herring, there's a way.

CHAPTER 15

"Zyzzogeton," I said and smiled at Mrs. Hargreaves.

"The last one?" she asked.

I nodded. We had at length reached the last word in Webster's New International Dictionary.

She sighed. "All right," she said, "give me the definition."

As I read her the definition of zyzzogeton, a South American leaf hopper with grooved tibiae, I could not help thinking how attractively grooved Mrs. Hargreaves' own tibiae were, but I put the thought resolutely from my mind. There was work to be done; I still had to count all the blocks in the city. This was no time for dalliance. Anyhow, all my attempts to couple with Mrs. Hargreaves had met with a conspicuous lack of success. I have described my first vain foray; there were many others, all failures. Although my persistence was not unaccompanied by ingenuity, her reactions were always negative. Even when I read aloud to her from *This Is My Beloved,* she remained unmoved.

But, like I said, this was no time for dalliance; there was work to be done. Mr. Atterbury had been patient—not to say uninterested—so far, but one never knew when he might pop in and expect his job to be done. And when one has a client as good as Mr. Atterbury, one tries to please him as well as one can. Especially when one has no other clients.

So without delay I put on good English walking shoes and a pair of tweed knickerbockers and set out on the second half of my assignment—counting all the blocks in the city. I started on the outskirts. My plan was to walk in concentric circles, spiraling inward until I had reached the center of town. For the first day or two I walked through almost rural surroundings. The houses were few and widely scattered, the streets were unpaved, wildflowers were rife, and dogs bit me freely. As my circles narrowed, the terrain became more and more citified. I was soon walking through streets of suburban houses. There was an occasional store, a hospital here and there, a few schools—including Wellfleet College. I single out Wellfleet College because of a curious story connected with that institution.

It seems that several years ago there was a young instructor at Wellfleet whose name was Selby Lake. Lake taught a course called psychology laboratory. The work in this course consisted of running white mice over mazes to see how rapidly they could learn to get from one end of the maze to the other. Students would stand by with notebooks and record the running time of the mice. Afterward the students would correlate and graph the data. This kind of work is something less than exciting, and anybody who had anything better to do kept away from psychology laboratory. Enrollment normally came to about twelve students.

In American colleges instructors who conduct popular and well-attended classes sometimes are paid as much as fifteen hundred dollars a year. Since Lake did not fall into this golden circle, he had to get along on far less. His wife, an attractive and economical young woman, did the best she could with her meager budget. Each night for dinner she served a meat loaf which was made with a large proportion of corn flakes. Often the meat loaf was all corn flakes and they ate it with sliced bananas.

Underpaid, undernourished, ill-clad, and ill-housed, Lake had still another cross to bear. His boss, Dean Stryker of the psychology department, was a man with a conviction that the only way to get good work out of his faculty was to keep them in constant terror of losing their jobs. Consequently, he never had a kind word for any of his instructors. In fact, he seldom spoke to them at all, but would just scowl and rumble in his throat when he met them.

One day—it was the beginning of a new semester—Lake stood in front of his class and tried to keep his teeth from chattering while he lectured. He was cold. Underneath his threadbare tweed jacket he was practically naked; his wife had made a dickey out of his frayed shirt and he had no underwear. Moreover, he was scared. Dean Stryker had just rumbled at him in the corridor before class. He was hungry, too. His breakfast had consisted of licking the tops of his neighbors' milk bottles.

But he steeled himself and went on to explain to his yawning audience of twelve what psychology laboratory was all about. Then he took six white mice out of a cage and marked each of them with a different colored dye—red, blue, green, black, yellow, and brown—so that the students could tell them apart. He put each mouse on the starting end of a maze. "The mice," he said, "have been trained to start running the mazes when I ring this bell on my desk. Are your notebooks ready? Here we go."

He struck the bell sharply and the mice scurried down the mazes.

Just as the mice began to run, one of the students nudged another one and said, "Hey, Bill, I'll bet you a dime on the red."

"You got a bet," replied the other.

Lake overheard this wager and made a mental note to tell his wife about it when he came home that evening, in the hope that it might brighten her bleak day. She was not, however, perceptibly cheered. "I wish *I* had a dime," was all she said.

Lake lay awake on his pallet far into that night. An idea had occurred to him—a wild, reckless, dangerous idea. At first he told himself that it was insane, that it could result only in catastrophe. But then he surveyed his current situation. "Could I," he asked himself, "be any worse off than I am now?" The answer, of course, was no.

So on the following morning, when his class was assembled, Lake cleared his throat nervously, and, with many misgivings, started to describe his plan. "Yesterday," he said, "I noticed that some of you were making bets on the mice. How would you like to make this practice a regular part of the curriculum?"

"Oh, marvy!" cried the students.

Encouraged, Lake went on. "I have known these mice for some time, and I am familiar with their running characteristics. Therefore I feel qualified to establish the odds on their chances of victory." He took a slip of paper out of his pocket and read from it. "I believe the following odds to be equitable: Red, 11 to 5; Blue, 3 to 1; Green, 8 to 1; Black, 8 to 5; Yellow, 17 to 20; Brown 15 to 1."

"Oh, terrif!" cried the students.

"If any of you should care to place a small bet before we start the first race—I mean experiment—will you kindly come up to my desk?"

As a man the students rose and rushed to the desk, waving handfuls of money. Lake gave each bettor a slip recording his choice, took the mice out of the cage, placed them on the mazes, and rang the bell.

They broke fast. Green took an early lead but was passed by Blue and Yellow at the halfway mark. Blue and Yellow ran neck and neck almost to the home stretch. Then suddenly Black started coming up fast on the outside. He caught up with the leaders on the last turn and pounded down to the finish line ahead by a whisker.

Lake made $6.85.

Lake's plan had been originally conceived as only an occasional thing. But when the students reported for class the next day, they insisted on doing it again. Nothing loath, Lake complied.

From that day on the psychology lab became a kind of indoor Hialeah. There were four races daily. Odds were posted on the blackboard before each race. Betting was expanded to include place and show wagers. An automatic camera was installed at the end of the mazes to record photo finishes. There were saliva tests, daily doubles, and tip sheets. Lake bought a checked suit.

News about Lake's class traveled quickly around the campus—not to the faculty, but to the other students. When the new semester rolled around, more than two hundred students registered for psychology laboratory. The lab was jammed to the walls, and the money rolled in.

One day shortly after the new semester had begun, Dean Stryker happened to glance at the enrollment figures for psychology laboratory. "By George," he said to himself, "this is odd. I think I'll drop in at young Lake's class and see what's going on."

He went out of his office and down the corridor to the lab. Just as he opened the door he heard a great shout of "They're off!" The students were crowded around the mazes, so engrossed in the race that they did not notice the dean's entrance. Nor did Lake.

The dean stood on tiptoe, craning his neck and watching the proceedings in openmouthed astonishment. The students' yells were deafening. "Come on, Red!" they shouted.

"Come on, Blue!" "Come on, Yellow!" "Come on, Brown!" They leaped up and down in a frenzy.

"By George," said the dean to himself, "no wonder enrollment is up. What a brilliant way to teach psychology laboratory—pretending that it's a horse race. I think I've underestimated young Lake."

The race ended. There were anguished howls from the losing bettors, cries of exultation from the winners. Above the din, Lake's voice could be heard: "Hurry, hurry, hurry! Place your bets. Next race goes on in ten minutes."

"By George," said the dean to himself, "this is remarkable. He's even got them pretending to make bets." Shaking his head in wonderment, the dean slipped from the room before the betting began. Nobody saw him go; nobody had seen him come.

Back in his office, the dean continued to shake his head. This, he thought, was far and away the most brilliant example he had ever seen of how to make a dull course interesting. What an inspiration! Pretending it was a horse race! With make-believe bets, yet!

"By George," said the dean to himself, "this Lake is a genius. Maybe, for once, I'll break my rule about never saying a kind word to the faculty. Yes, by George, I'll do it. I'll call Lake in here this afternoon and say something nice to him.

"But not *too* nice," added the dean to himself. "Can't have him getting cocky."

So that afternoon the dean called Lake into his office. Lake stood in front of the dean's desk, his heart beating wildly. Never before had he been called into this august chamber. It could only mean trouble.

"Lake," said the dean, "I looked in on your class this morning." He paused for a moment, thinking of something

That ought to do it, he thought.

nice to say, but not too nice. At length he had it. "Mighty interesting," he said.

The dean leaned back in his swivel chair and folded his hands over his paunch. That ought to do it, he thought. Nice, but not too nice.

The color drained out of Lake's head. The worst had happened; the dean knew his secret. He trembled at a sudden vision of prison gates and rock piles. He looked at the dean, and his trembling increased. No hope of mercy in that hard, silent face. The jig was up.

"Well?" croaked Lake.

The dean blinked. "Well what?"

"What else are you going to say?"

"That's all," replied the dean angrily. He cursed himself for having broken his rule. See what happens? You give these fellows one kind word and they want a testimonial. "Go," he commanded.

Lake scratched his head. This made no sense whatever. Bewildered, he turned away. As he took his first step his shoe became entangled in a worn spot in the rug. He tripped and almost fell.

"Confound that rug!" shouted the dean. "I've been after the college for ten years to get me a new one. I'd buy it myself if I could afford it."

"Ah," said Lake.

Everything was suddenly clear to him. So that was the dean's game, was it? Well, he'd play along. He flashed the dean a quick wink. "Got you," he said and went out of the office.

"Did that fellow wink at me?" the dean asked himself incredulously. "No," he replied firmly. "He wouldn't dare."

A day later the dean received a beautiful Persian rug. Attached was a card that said simply, "Compliments of a Friend." The dean, of course, could not imagine who had sent it, but he was never one to look a gift horse in the mouth. He had the rug laid and said no more.

Several weeks later—it was a freezing-cold winter afternoon—the dean went out to the campus parking lot to get his car and go home. It was a very old car, and when the dean tried to start it, the motor wouldn't even turn over. Raging, he got out and began to crank. Vainly he spun the crank over and over, his anger mounting with each turn.

He was standing and kicking his car in a fury of frustration when Lake happened to walk by. "Hiya, Dean," said Lake pleasantly. "Anything the matter?"

"I'll tell you what's the matter," roared the dean, his eyes blazing at Lake. "I've got to have a new car."

Lake paled. "Gee, I don't know," he said doubtfully. "That's a lot of money."

"I know it's a lot of money, you idiot," thundered the Dean. "But I've got to have one."

Lake shrugged. "Okay, okay," he muttered and walked away. So it's a car now, he thought unhappily. And what will it be next time? Still, what could he do? So the following morning there was a brand-new sedan in front of the dean's house. "Compliments of a Friend," said a card on the steering wheel.

Again the dean chose not to look a gift horse in the mouth.

This whole singular combination of circumstances came to a head on New Year's Eve at the Faculty Club Ball. It was a tradition of the college for all members of the faculty and their wives to attend this annual event. The Lakes had never been able to afford it in previous years, but this time they made a truly splendid appearance—Lake in faultlessly tailored tails, Mrs. Lake in gold lamé, a diamond choker, and an ermine wrap.

Dean Stryker had never before seen Mrs. Lake, and he was impressed. At first he admired her in silence, but later in the evening, made genial by several drinks, he decided to speak. He lifted a finger and beckoned Lake to his side.

"Excuse me," said Lake to his wife. "I've got to go talk to the dean."

"What do you suppose he wants?" asked Mrs. Lake.

"Plenty, if I know the old hog," answered Lake bitterly. "I'll be right back."

He crossed the room to the dean's side. "Well, what now?" he asked uneasily.

"That wife of yours," said the dean. "Mighty attractive woman."

Lake's eyes popped out in horrified disbelief. "No!" he whispered hoarsely. And then the whisper became a roar of rage. "No, damn you! This time you've gone too far!"

With that he smote the dean on the nose with all his force, wheeled, went back to his wife, took her by the arm, strode out, and was never heard from again.

Years have gone by since the disappearance of Selby Lake. Psychology laboratory is again a dull, ill-attended class. The dean's new car is old, and his rug is getting threadbare. He has long since stopped wondering who gave him the car and the rug; he is satisfied now that the mystery will never be solved. But he still thinks occasionally about Selby Lake. He blames himself for Lake's insanity. (Insanity is the only reason the dean can imagine for Lake's conduct.) "I should never," says the dean frequently to himself, "have spoken kindly to him. He went crazy with joy."

CHAPTER 16

But I digress. I was telling about how I counted the blocks for Payson Atterbury.

Well, sir, I started on the outskirts of town, walked through the suburbs and residential sections, and finally ended up in the commercial district. One day when I was walking down Market Street, a dingy thoroughfare which runs along the tracks on the edge of downtown, who should I bump into but George Overmeyer. "George, you old sonofagun," I cried in my bluff, hale manner.

"Hello, Harry. What are you doing down here?"

Mindful of Mr. Atterbury's admonition not to reveal my connection with him, I replied, "Oh, I'm just out for a breath of fresh air." This was perhaps not the most brilliant of evasions, since there were two tanneries across the street. "But what are *you* doing down here?" I countered.

He pointed to a warehouse a few doors away. ROSSI

WHOLESALE LIQUOR CO. said a sign on the side of the building. "I've got to buy some booze. Want to come along?"

"Charmed," I said and accompanied him into the warehouse. It was a dank, cavernous place, jammed with ceiling-high stacks of whisky cases. George took me over to a roll-top desk in the corner of the warehouse and introduced me to Mr. Rossi, a swarthy, scar-faced man in a derby hat and purple suit.

"Hiya, Jack," said Mr. Rossi to me.

"I want to order some whisky," said George.

"Got cash?" asked Rossi.

"No," said George, "but I'll pay you in a week or so."

"Cash," said Rossi. "Now."

"I don't get it," said George. "Haven't I always paid you?"

"Yeah, but it's gettin' slower and slower," replied Rossi.

"Look, Rossi," said George, "you know I've got a good business."

What George said was perfectly true. Everybody in Ivanhoe Gardens bought their liquor from him, and Ivanhoe Gardens was what you might call a drinking community. A neighborhood statistician once figured out that the glass used in the bottles of whisky consumed annually in Ivanhoe Gardens would be sufficient to replace every window in the Pentagon. He did not say what effect brown window glass would have on the already shaky morale of Pentagon employees.

"Sure you got a good business," Rossi admitted. "But

Mr. Rossi

look how you run it. You come in for ten minutes every day, rifle the till, and then go out to the track and lose the dough. You're no credit risk. You're a bum."

"Well, how do you like that?" said George, turning to me in amazement. "Rossi calls me a bum. *Rossi!* Did you ever hear of this guy during prohibition, Harry? Murderer, thug, bootlegger, racketeer . . ."

A dreamy look came into Rossi's eyes. "Yeh," he breathed. "Murderer, thug, bootlegger, racketeer . . . Pimp, too. And numbers, kidnaping, hijacking, arson, smuggling. Ah," he sighed, "them was the days. Remember the time I hijacked the drug company truck? I thought it was loaded with medical alcohol. Turned out to be bubble bath. I spiked it and sold it for sparkling burgundy.

"And remember," he chuckled, "the Elm Street Massacre? Killed forty-seven guys and six elms.

"Ah, them was the days," he sighed again. He shook his head reminiscently for a moment and then turned to George. "But now I'm a businessman and I say you're a bum."

George argued some more, but Rossi kept shaking his head and saying "Cash," so we finally left.

"You haven't got any money you can lend me, have you, Harry?" asked George when we were back on the street.

"I'm sorry, George, I haven't," I replied. "Why don't you try a bank?"

"If Rossi thinks I'm a bum," said George, "what will a bank think?"

"You've got a point," I allowed. "Well, George, I'll scout

around and see if I can find some money for you— Say!" I cried, struck with a sudden thought. "Why don't you go see Payson Atterbury? Bad risks are his business."

George smiled. "Walk down the street with me for a minute. I want to show you something." We walked a little way and came to Nick's shoeshine stand. "See this?" asked George. "A couple of years ago Nick needed fifty cents to buy a new shoeshine rag. Atterbury lent him the money. Now Nick is working for Atterbury.

"Come on." He took me a few steps farther—to Sam's Café. "Last year Sam wanted to buy a mimeograph machine to print his menus. He borrowed the money from Atterbury. Now Atterbury owns the restaurant.

"What's more," said George, taking me on to Wang Lin's Chinese laundry next door, "Atterbury repossessed the mimeograph machine and sold it to Wang Lin for a mangle."

We were at the corner. "I'll leave you now," said George, "with these words of wisdom: Never do business with Payson Atterbury."

George turned the corner and I continued down Market Street, smiling to myself. Never do business with Payson Atterbury, indeed! There was nobody I would rather do business with. Mr. Atterbury was the nicest, sweetest, kindest man I knew. So what if he drove a hard bargain? That did not make him a villain. What George failed to realize was that some of our greatest citizens, our most generous philanthropists, were hard bargainers when it came to business. Take Andrew Carnegie. Nobody has ever claimed that he was softhearted in a business deal, and yet without his generosity hundreds of American cities would today be without libraries and the works of Zane Grey would be unknown to millions.

Someday, I thought as I walked, George would realize the basic kindliness of Payson Atterbury. Then the two would be friends. Mr. Atterbury, I knew, was already amiably disposed toward George, for he was always asking me about him. Only George needed to be won over. Perhaps I would be the man to do it. It was to be hoped; nothing would give me greater pleasure than to bring these two fine gentlemen, my best friends, together in comradeship.

This I thought as I counted the blocks.

CHAPTER 17

"A party, a party, we're gonna have a party!" I sang merrily—but softly, lest Miss Geddes become angry and change her mind. It was only after a great deal of wheedling that she had consented to the party. For weeks I had been reminding her that we had to reciprocate for all the times we had been entertained by our neighbors, and finally she agreed.

I must confess that I was being devilish sly. It wasn't really out of obligation to our friends that I urged the party; it was because I wanted to play host. For a long time I had felt myself capable of performing this function. I had the poise, the background, and Dad Geddes's black velvet jacket with frogs for buttons.

But as the day of the party approached, I grew increasingly nervous. Perhaps I was rushing things. I had, to be sure, won my spurs in Ivanhoe Gardens society—but as a guest, not as a host. It is one thing to go to a party, quite another to give one. Did I, I wondered, really, truly, honestly have the stuff?

My fears were groundless. As soon as the first couple arrived, my jitters vanished abruptly. "Good evening, good evening, good evening!" I cried jovially, pumping their hands and giving them funny hats to wear. "Wow-dow!" I shouted. "Sure gonna be some doin's here tonight!" Winking broadly, I pinched the lady's bottom and bade them enter.

Nor did my charm diminish as the other guests arrived. To each I gave a cheery greeting that made him feel not just welcome, but *wanted.* This to me is the essence of hospitality. It is well enough to be polite to a guest, to see that he has plenty to eat and drink, but a true host will do more. He will make each guest feel that his (the guest's) presence is absolutely essential to his (the host's) happiness. This feeling I endeavored to instill in all my guests, and to make sure that I had succeeded, I sobbed piteously when each finally went home.

When the guests were all assembled, I clapped my hands for attention and announced that we were all going to play Twenty Questions. "Shove it," said Miss Geddes, and the others gaily echoed her sentiments. Nor were they any more receptive to my proposals of Pin the Tail on the Donkey, Going to Jerusalem, or Authors. For these were people who did not need games or any such artificial stimuli to keep a party bubbling. Conversationalists to a man, filled with *savoir-faire* and *joie de vivre,* they required nothing besides themselves and liquor to make an evening a success. Until dawn the good talk flowed, sometimes serious, sometimes frivolous, always engrossing.

Out of the many interesting conversations that night, a few stay particularly in my mind. One was Mr. Bergen's account of his trip to Europe. Mr. Bergen, an eminent bath-towel jobber, had just completed a six-day junket to London, Paris, Rome, and the Riviera, so he knew whereof he spoke.

"The most outstanding feature of London," said Mr. Bergen, "is the bad teeth of the natives."

"What can you expect with a Labor government?" said Mr. Atterbury.

"The English policemen are called bobbies, after Sir Robert Peel who founded the English police force," said Mr. Bergen.

"Isn't that interesting?" said George Overmeyer. "The American police are called cops, after Sir Robert Coppers who founded the American police force."

"I didn't know that," said Mr. Bergen. He continued: "On the grounds of Windsor Castle is the famous Queen's Doll House. The manufacturers of Great Britain presented it to the Queen Mother Mary several years ago. It stands about ten feet high and has fifteen rooms, each completely furnished. All the furnishings in the little house actually work. There's a little piano that can be played, a little stove that cooks, a little washing machine that washes—everything really works. The paintings on the wall are miniatures done by England's greatest artists. The little books in the library are real books, printed in type that can be read with a magnifying glass."

"I think it's a dirty shame making that poor old queen live in that little tiny house," said Mrs. Overmeyer.

"Do you think," asked Mr. Atterbury, "that France is going communist?"

"I'm glad you asked that question," said Mr. Bergen. "When I was in Paris I made it a point to talk to the man in the street, to find out which way their political sentiments are trending."

"Is it true," interrupted Mrs. Overmeyer, "that in Paris there are lady attendants in the men's washrooms?"

"Yes," replied Mr. Bergen. "Now, as I was saying, I went out and took, you might call it, an unofficial poll. In fact, I did the same thing in Rome."

"Do they have them there too?" asked Mrs. Overmeyer.

"What?" said Mr. Bergen.

"Lady attendants in the men's washrooms."

"I don't really know," answered Mr. Bergen. "To tell you the truth, I wasn't in Rome long enough to go to the washroom. . . . But to get back to Atterbury's question, let me give you an illustration. I hired a car in Paris. Fellow named Jacques drove it."

"What an odd name for a Frenchman," remarked George Overmeyer.

"They have the goddamdest names," replied Mr. Bergen. "Well, sir, I had many a talk with my friend Jacques."

"Can they see what you're doing?" asked Mrs. Overmeyer.

"Who?" said Mr. Bergen.

"The lady attendants in the men's washrooms."

"Yes, I believe they can. But, as I was saying, this Jacques——"

"I'd be too embarrassed to do anything," I giggled.

"This fellow Jacques," Mr. Bergen went on, "was what you might call a typical Frenchman—four feet eight inches tall and a pervert."

"Are there men attendants in the ladies' washrooms?" asked Mrs. Overmeyer.

"I couldn't say," replied Mr. Bergen.

"It's only fair," said Mrs. Overmeyer.

"Perhaps. . . . Well, to get back to Jacques, I said to him one day, 'Jacques, let's forget that I'm an American and you're a Frenchman. I want you to consider yourself an equal for the moment.' "

"A handsome gesture," said George Overmeyer. "Now we're even for the Statue of Liberty."

"Well, I believe that every American who goes to Europe should think of himself as a kind of ambassador," said Mr. Bergen. "Try to build good will. Be friendly. Be tolerant. Keep your disgust to yourself."

"These women in the men's washrooms," said Mrs. Overmeyer. "Do they get paid?"

Reluctantly I took my leave at this point. I had spent quite a little time conversing with this group, and I was afraid that the other guests might feel themselves unwanted if I did not also devote some time to them. With a cheery smile I went over and joined a group of ladies. Here the conversation was not of such global significance; it was, in fact, just an exchange of friendly gossip about some of our neighbors. I put my hand on Miss Geddes's shoulder and listened. (The hand was withdrawn shortly after she burned it with a cigarette.)

"I understand that Beatrice Venable's hair is dyed," said Mrs. Oxnard.

"That's not true," said Mrs. Herwig, springing to Beatrice Venable's defense. "It's a wig."

"That's right," said Mrs. Flandrau. "Sam shaved her head after he caught her with the Japanese gardener."

"Sam's a fine one to go around shaving heads," said Mrs. Westlake. "Remember the way he carried on with the Swedish maid at the Bascombs' house that night?"

"Well, so did all the other men," said Mrs. Richards.

"A regular smörgåsbord," I giggled.

"The Bascombs take dope, don't they?" said Mrs. Hershey.

"I wouldn't be surprised," said Mrs. Atterbury. "I know their silverware is plated."

"I will say this for the Bascombs," said Mrs. Wycliff. "Helen certainly knows how to dress. Did you see her at the symphony last week? I've never seen her looking so young."

"No wonder," said Mrs. Kingsley. "That was her confirmation dress."

"Did you see Mildred Worthington at the symphony with that Goldberg boy?" said Mrs. Daley. "She looked absolutely exhausted."

"Those Jews are so passionate," said Mrs. Cheever. "I wonder why."

"Because they can't get into country clubs," explained Mrs. Howe.

Much as I would have liked to stay and hear some more friendly gossip, I felt it my duty to move on to some other guests before they began to feel that I was neglecting them. I joined a group of men gathered at the bar. Here the topic was one of keen interest to all us middle-classmates: income taxes.

"I hear Jack Benson's in trouble with the Internal Revenue people," said Mr. Daley.

"Wha' hoppen?" said Mr. Hernandez.

"Remember that miscarriage Jack's wife had three years ago?" said Mr. Daley. "Well, Jack's listing it as a dependent."

"I tell you," said Mr. Richards, "income taxes are going to be the ruin of this country."

"That's right," said Mr. Westlake. "There's no risk capital any more. Nobody wants to take a chance."

"Why should they?" said Mr. Flandrau. "The government takes all your profits."

"Right," said Mr. Kingsley. "Nobody's going to expand or branch out unless he can make some money."

"Taxes have taken all the incentive out of business," said Mr. Olin.

"The whole economy is shrinking," said Mr. Wycliff.

All nodded and sighed.

"Well, Daley," said Mr. Westlake, "how's that branch office of yours coming along?"

"Be open next month," said Mr. Daley. "Say, I hear you bought the building next door to your store."

"That's right," said Mr. Westlake. "I'm going to bust out the wall and double my floor space."

"I'll be calling on you," said Mr. Richards. "We're putting in three new lines of merchandise down at the warehouse."

"Then I'll be calling on *you,*" said Mr. Flandrau. "My garage has branched out into the truck business now too."

"Better call on me too," said Mr. Olin. "I'm opening a string of stores out in the suburbs."

It was time again for me to move on to some more guests. Shaking my head sadly because income taxes had destroyed all incentive for business to expand, I turned away and started for a group singing "Sweet Violets" at the piano. My clear alto was more than welcome, even though I did not know the lyrics.

From the singers I went to another group and then to another and another and another, brightening the corners where they were. Nobody, I took pains to assure, was deprived of my presence this night.

The sun was well over the horizon when the last guests crawled out to their car. Tired but happy, I sank into an easy chair and reviewed the evening. By any standard, it had been a swimming success. I had passed my first test as host with flying colors; not a man jack of my guests had complained about feeling unwanted. How proud, I thought, Miss Geddes must be of me. Perhaps even proud enough to——

I leaped from the chair and raced around the house looking for her. I found her at last underneath the bar, curled peacefully on the floor, a bottle of champagne in her hand. Gently, so as not to wake her, I picked her up and carried her to her room, the champagne bottle still dangling from her hand. I laid her carefully on her bed, then tiptoed over to the window and lowered the blinds. On tiptoe I returned to her. Gently I started to pull the champagne bottle out of her hand. Sleeping, she held tighter to the bottle. I increased my pressure, and the cork flew out with a report like a pistol shot.

She sat bolt upright in bed. "What do you want?" she demanded.

"Aw, you know," I answered.

"Get the hell out of here," she said.

"No," I said, determination rising within me. "No, Miss Geddes, I will not get out," I said grittily. "I will not allow this marriage to be made a mockery of any longer. I know my rights."

She looked at me for a long time and then took a pull on the bottle of champagne. "All right," she shrugged.

"Oh, boy!" I cried and started to undo the frogs on Dad Geddes's jacket.

"But put the cat out first," she said.

"Yes, ma'am," I said.

I picked her up and carried her to her room.

I flew on wings of love to put Tabby outside. What Tabby? We didn't have a cat, I suddenly remembered as I reached the foot of the stairs. By the time I got back up, Miss Geddes's door was bolted.

Little minx.

CHAPTER 18

"Mr. Atterbury to see you, stud," said Mrs. Hargreaves.

"Show him in! Show him in!" I cried. I leaped up and wrung my client's hand as he entered my office. "Just in time, sir. I have only this minute finished my assignment. There it is."

I pointed to a stack of typewritten pages that stood next to, and slightly higher than, the filing cabinet. "Come see," I invited.

But Mr. Atterbury only nodded absently. There was a look of great distress on his face. "Is anything the matter, sir?" I inquired, taking his hands in mine.

"It's George Overmeyer," he said hoarsely and shook with silent sobs.

"What's happened to him?"

"It's too terrible," said Mr. Atterbury. He sat down for a moment and composed himself. "His business is on the verge of collapse. He has no liquor left and he can't get credit to buy more."

"I didn't realize it had gone that far," I said, shocked. "I knew he was in trouble. He asked me to lend him some money not long ago."

"You didn't, did you?" asked Mr. Atterbury sharply.

"No, sir. I suggested that he borrow from you, but he said you were a stinker."

"I know," sighed Mr. Atterbury. "He has some delusion that I'm not an honorable man. I don't know where he ever got such an idea."

"Beats hell out of me," I confessed.

"Well, no matter," said my client. "Even if George doesn't like me, I like him and I want to help him."

I blinked back a tear.

"George has a fine business," he continued. "That store makes a lot of money. But he, the stupid bastard, loses it all at the races. Poor, misguided soul," he added tenderly.

I sighed.

"But I think he's learned his lesson now. I think if somebody lent him the money to make a fresh start, he'd buckle down and make a go of the business. I want to lend him the money. I don't care what he says or thinks about me, I want to do this for him."

I groped for words to express my admiration of this greatheartedness, but none came.

"And I don't even want any interest on the money, just a nominal amount—say 2 per cent—to make it legal."

I turned my back so he could not see the tears streaming down my cheeks.

"I just want to rehabilitate George, to make him a useful, self-respecting member of society. That's what I want."

I snatched up the telephone on my desk. "Mr. Atterbury, I'm going to call him this minute and tell him everything you've said."

"No, you cretin!" he screamed, yanking the telephone out of my hand. "I mean," he went on in a gentler tone, "that isn't the way to do it. George, for some obscure reason, doesn't trust me. He'd never accept any help from me."

He put his arm around my shoulder. "You, Harry, are going to lend him the money."

"I, sir?"

"Yes. I'll give you the money and you'll give it to George. You must let him think that it's your own. You must never, never mention my name, or the whole thing won't work. Keep me out of it. You take all the credit."

To be charitable is admirable. To be charitable anonymously is doubly admirable. But to be charitable anonymously and deliberately let another take the credit is admirable beyond even my vast powers to describe. I flung myself on the divan and wept without shame.

"There, there," said Mr. Atterbury, cradling me in his arms. "There, there."

At length I collected myself. "I will do as you say, sir," I declared. "I will keep your noble secret."

We shook hands silently, not trusting ourselves to speak.

"Now, listen," said Mr. Atterbury when the charged moment was over. "We're not only going to rescue George from his present predicament. We're going to make him a bigger, richer, more important man than he ever dreamed. I have plans for his business."

"Do you mean," I asked incredulously, "that lending him money is not the extent of your generosity? Do you mean that you also are going to contribute your tremendous business acumen to George's problem?"

He lowered his eyes modestly, but seized me before I could hurl myself on the divan again.

"Listen carefully, Harry. You've got to remember all this. Now, when you go to see George, this is what you'll tell him . . ."

"George," I said, "I've got all the money you need and I want to lend it to you."

George looked at me curiously. "Where'd you get it?"

"I have sources," I said with an inscrutable smile.

"How much interest?" he asked.

"A nominal amount—say 2 per cent—to make it legal."

George scratched his chin. "Then it can't be from Atterbury," he said. "Now let me get this straight. You've got money and you're going to lend it to me at 2 per cent. Why?"

"What are friends for?" I said simply.

George looked at me closely for a long time. "What do you want for collateral?"

"Only the assurance that you'll mend your ways," I replied.

"Huh?"

"George, I have investigated your business very thoroughly. It's a good, sound business. In the last quarter your volume was nearly ninety thousand dollars. Your gross profit ran close to eighteen thousand dollars. Your net profit was a little over seven thousand dollars—at least it would have been if you'd left it in the register. Right?"

George nodded dumbly.

"That's a very good business, not a business to milk and neglect. George, if I lend you the money, I want a guarantee that from now on you're going to come to the store every morning, work all day, see that it's properly run, and stop rifling the cash register. You've got to reform, old friend. I'm not going to lend you the money if you go back to your bad habits."

"Look, Harry, I don't want to seem ungrateful, but this is so strange. You want a guarantee that I'll be a good boy. What kind of guarantee?"

"Simply this. I'll put you on a three-month trial period. At the end of that time if the store doesn't show a profit it belongs to me."

"And if it does show a profit?"

"Then it's yours forever. You can pay me back the loan whenever you like. Ten years—twenty years, if you want."

George got up and paced back and forth silently. At last he stopped. "Harry," he said earnestly, "if this is a swindle, please don't do it. It would be like shooting birds on the ground. I don't know my butt from my elbow when it comes to business. Anybody with an ounce of larceny can pauperize me."

"A swindle!" I cried. For a moment I was angry. "This is the most decent thing one human being has ever done for another."

"But these things don't happen in business."

"It's happening now."

"You're quite sure you're not giving me the finger?"

"No, George, the hand. The helping hand. Unlimited credit. All the money you need. Why, you haven't even scratched the surface with your liquor store. You're going to get bigger, better, richer."

"How? I've got all the business in Ivanhoe Gardens now."

"But Ivanhoe Gardens isn't the whole city. You have delivery trucks. You could sell your liquor all over town. Run big ads in the papers. Compete with the downtown stores. Cut prices."

"But I don't operate on that scale."

"That's right, you don't. You're small-time now. But things are going to be different. No more ordering a few measly cases at a time from Rossi. Who needs Rossi anyhow? Cut out the middleman. Order car lots direct from the distillery."

I leaped up and strode back and forth, waving my arms. "You're going to get big, George," I declared. "All you have to do is to start thinking big. Buy big. Sell big. Volume, volume, volume—that's the secret. You'll be a millionaire, George—a multimillionaire."

"What the hell have you been smoking?"

"English Ovals, but I think I'm going to change. I've got a cigarette holder now and they won't fit. Why?"

"Harry, try to concentrate. What do *you* get out of all this?"

"The thrill of helping a friend in need. I'm going to help, George. Not just with the money. I'm going to help with the business—buying, selling, advertising, everything."

"For nothing?"

"Let us say," I suggested with a warm smile, "for love."

George examined me as minutely as a specimen under a microscope. "There is no guile," he said, "in your vapid face. Your brain is incapable of the sustained thought required for commercial highbindery. You are always sincere even when uttering the veriest crap . . . Harry, I trust you. It's a deal."

I clasped his hand.

"And, Harry," he said with a shy grin, "thanks."

"My pleasure."

"If there is ever anything I can do for you——"

"Nothing, nothing."

"I'll see if I can find you an oval cigarette holder," he said.

CHAPTER 19

Talk about excitement!

First Mr. Atterbury calls me and says he's got a line on a thousand cases of Old Popskull that can be picked up for practically nothing. I call George—pretending, of course, that I've made the discovery myself. "I think we ought to grab them," I tell George, and he replies, "Anything you say, pal."

So we buy a thousand cases of Old Popskull. Then it turns out that George hasn't got room for them in his store. Fortunately I am able to rent a warehouse from Mr. Atterbury. Then I take an ad in the *Daily News*. Aware of the effectiveness of white space in advertising, I buy a full page and have just these few words printed in small type in the center:

OLD POPSKULL—$3.99

It is a striking ad. When I see a proof of it, I am so overcome with admiration that I overlook the fact I have neglected to mention the name of George's store.

George calls the omission to my attention after the ad appears in the paper, and we have a good chuckle. The next morning we run the ad again, this time including the name of George's store. Well, sir, the orders pour in all morning and George's trucks speed madly around town delivering Old Popskull. This activity ceases suddenly at two o'clock, when the afternoon papers hit the street. They all carry ads of the big downtown liquor stores, cutting Old Popskull to $3.95, to $3.89, even to $3.75.

George calls me. "What do I do now?" he asks.

"Let me think," I reply.

I call Mr. Atterbury. "What do I do now?" I ask.

"Cut the price," says Mr. Atterbury.

I call George. "I've got it," I say. "Cut the price."

We cut to $3.59, to $3.29, to $2.98, to $2.49. Each time the downtown stores undercut us, we undercut them right back. My blood is tingling with the excitement of the contest. At last I understand the romance and adventure of business. It is as though I am the chief of staff of an army engaged in an arduous campaign. George is my field commander. Mr. Atterbury is the President of the United States.

George calls me one day. "Harry," he says, "the way I've got it figured, I'm losing $1.23 on each bottle of Old Popskull."

"Let me think," I say.

I call Mr. Atterbury and report.

He tells me to forget about the Old Popskull campaign, for he has just made a deal with twelve unfrocked Benedictine monks to buy all their output. "I'm getting it for a song," he says.

"For a Gregorian chant, you mean," I reply, giggling.

"Call George," says Mr. Atterbury.

I call George and we order the unfrocked Benedictine. A few days later Mr. Atterbury is able to get his hands on a car of bargain rye. Later he finds scotch, bourbon, wine, gin, and cordials at prices we can't possibly pass up. We have to rent another warehouse from him.

I continue to write the ads, but I start planning them more carefully. I seek for some unique feature, some felicitous phrase, something to make the ads really arresting. No good thoughts come to me. I decide to consult a word expert—Wrose Wrigley.

I go to her home and state my problem. "Can you help me?" I ask.

"Of course I can, Harrykins," she replies. "But let's get comfortable first."

"Later," I say, for I know she is inclined to sluggishness after union.

"First," she insists, and I have no choice but to comply.

Spirits of ammonia fail to revive her. She is too heavy to drag to the shower, so I pull the garden hose in through the window and run a cold jet on her. Then I towel her until she glows dully, and we sit down to work.

She turns out some mighty catchy jingles for my ads. Here's one:

Fishes, they have tails and fins.
Ragweeds, they have pollens.
Overmeyer's has the gins
That make the best Tom Collins.

Here's another one:

Overmeyer's sells Three Feathers.
Overmeyer's sells Park and Tilford.
You couldn't get them any cheaper
Unless you went out in the dark and pilfered.

In the face of the crushing cleverness of our ads, our competitors quail. They do not, however, give up. They undercut our prices. We undercut theirs. They undercut ours again.

George confesses to a growing feeling of uneasiness. "You sure you know what you're doing?" he keeps asking me.

"Of course, of course!" I roar jovially and phone Mr. Atterbury for instructions.

Mr. Atterbury is like a rock. "Cut prices," he says. "Buy more liquor," he says. "Cut prices," he says. "Buy more liquor," he says.

I hustle and bustle. George worries and scurries.

And the three months pass as swiftly as three hours. For me they are three wonderful months—exciting months, tingling months, exhilarating months, electrifying months. In short, businessmen's months.

CHAPTER 20

I stood looking out of my office window. A soft snow had fallen the night before, and now the streets glistened with fairyland brightness. The holly wreaths hanging on the lampposts were tinged with white; frost streaked the gaily decked windows of the stores. Christmas shoppers, heavy laden with packages, thronged the sidewalks. They pushed and jostled merrily, calling the greetings of the season to each other. The sound of caroling came out of the music stores, and passers-by paused to listen and, occasionally, to join in.

I turned and sat down at my desk, full of peace on earth, good will to men, and the spirit of giving. My Christmas shopping was all done. I had bought a handsomely packaged aphrodisiac for Miss Geddes. For Mother I had bought a three-year subscription to her trade journal

—*The Scrubwoman's Home Companion.* For Dad I had bought one thousand three-cent stamps. (Dad—clever man!—was now engaged in a scheme that was sure to bring about the return of men's caps. It was a hellishly ingenious switch on the old chain-letter plan. Dad was sending letters to people all over the country. Each letter contained a list of ten names. The recipient of the letter was instructed to send a cap to the name at the head of the list, put his own name at the end of the list, and then mail copies of the letter to ten friends. Dad figured to have twenty million caps in circulation by the end of winter.)

I sat at my desk, basking in Yuletide cheer, and my mind turned to a lovely old Christmas story that had been a favorite of my youth. "The Gift of the Magi," it was called. There is also, I am told, a story of O. Henry's by that name. The one I was thinking of was by F. Henry and quite a different tale. In F. Henry's story there is a young couple named——

"Mr. Atterbury to see you," said Mrs. Hargreaves, interrupting my reverie.

I rose with a warm smile. "How fitting that you should arrive at this moment," I told my client as he entered the office. "I was just sitting here thinking about Christmas, and here you are—Santa Claus."

"And here is one of my reindeer," said Mr. Atterbury, pointing to a small, bald man with a brief case who had entered behind him. "Mr. Riddle, Mr. Young."

"Now, isn't that a coincidence!" I exclaimed. "I was just

thinking about a story in which the hero's name is Young—Jim Young."

"Yatata, yatata," said Mr. Young. He sat down and opened his brief case. "Come on already. My time is money."

"Mr. Young is your accountant," explained Mr. Atterbury.

"Really? I didn't know I had one," I confessed.

"Oh yes," said Mr. Atterbury. "In fact, Mr. Young has just finished a big job for you—an audit of George Overmeyer's books to see if George showed a profit in the first three months. You remember the agreement, of course."

"Of course," I said. "This story I was telling you about is called 'The Gift of the Magi.' Are you familiar with it?"

"Sure, it's O. Henry's," said Mr. Atterbury. "Now you listen to Mr. Young. He's going to read you the figures."

"Overmeyer's Liquor Store. Quarterly report," Mr. Young read from a large balance sheet. "Total sales—$183,-064.35."

"Wonderful!" I said, pleased. "It used to be only $90,000. It's more than doubled. . . . You're wrong about that story, P.A. It's not O. Henry's; it's F. Henry's. It's about this poor New York couple, Jim and Della Young. They're very poor and very much in love and it's Christmas Eve and they haven't got any money to buy presents for one another. Della is at home wondering how she can raise some money to buy Jim a Christmas present before he gets back from work. It looks impossible, but suddenly she gets an idea. She has beautiful long hair that hangs down almost to her knees. She's terribly proud of her hair, but she loves Jim so much that she decides to sell her hair to a wigmaker in order to get money to buy Jim a watch chain. Jim, you see, has a very fine old watch, and he's very proud of it, but he hasn't got a chain for it. So she goes to a wigmaker and he cuts off her hair and gives her twenty dollars and she buys a beautiful platinum chain for Jim's watch."

"Gross profit—$17,986.47," said Mr. Young.

"Hm," I said with some surprise. "Gross profit used to be $18,000. Now, with more than twice the volume, it shows a four-dollar drop."

"That," explained Mr. Atterbury, "is because he cut the prices of his liquor so much."

I scratched my head. "But buying liquor in those huge quantities—didn't that reduce the cost a great deal?"

"To be sure," replied Mr. Atterbury. "But you're forgetting warehouse charges. Rent, insurance, night watchmen—those things add up."

"Of course," I said. "How silly of me. Now, where was I? Oh yes. Jim gets home from work and Della gives him the watch chain. Then it develops that he has sold the watch to buy her a set of fancy combs for her hair. Only now, of course, she hasn't got the hair because she's sold it to buy him a chain for his watch. But he hasn't got the watch any more. Well, sir, they have a good cry and then a good laugh and then they fall into each other's arms with many a hug and kiss."

"That's O. Henry's story," said Mr. Atterbury.

"Operating expenses—$16,249.79," said Mr. Young.

"Whew!" I whistled. "That's up nearly $6000 over what it used to be."

"Advertising," said Mr. Atterbury.

"Of course," I said. "How silly of me. . . . You're wrong, P.A. It's not O. Henry's story. Wait till I finish it. You'll see. Now, everything goes along just dandy between Jim and Della for a few months. Then one day she's downtown shopping and she sees a man standing outside of a store. He's an ugly little bowlegged man in his late fifties, dressed in a horrible, flashy suit. Della, since she met Jim, has never even looked at another man, and even if she had, she wouldn't have chosen this repulsive little man in the flashy suit. And yet there is something about him that attracts her so strongly that she can't take her eyes off of him. She doesn't know what it is, but there is something about this man that draws her with unbelievable strength. She just stands there and stares at him in utter fascination.

"After a while the little man notices her staring. He leers and walks over and takes her arm. Her flesh creeps at his touch. All her instincts tell her to scream or strike him or run away or call a policeman. But she can't move. There's something about him that leaves her completely helpless. 'Do you live around here, babe?' he asks, and she nods dumbly. 'Let's go, then,' he says, and without volition, as though in a dream, she takes him to her flat and submits to his loathsome caresses.

"He keeps coming back every day when Jim is at work

Although she finds him nauseating and is profoundly disgusted by the whole sordid mess, she is absolutely powerless. The attraction of this little man, whatever it is, simply destroys her will."

She couldn't take her eyes off him.

"Will you, for Christ's sake," yelled Mr. Young, "let me finish and get out of here?"

"But I thought you were finished," I said truthfully. "Gross profit is $17,986.47. Subtract operating expenses—$16,249.79—and you get a net profit of $1736.68. It's not much, but at least it's a profit." I smiled. "George will be so relieved to know the store is safely his. I'm going to wait till Christmas to tell him the good news. It will make such a nice present. . . . And now, to finish my story——"

"Harry," said Mr. Atterbury, "Mr. Young has one more item."

"In a minute," I said. "Let me finish first. . . . The little man keeps coming around to Della's flat every day for several months, and then he begins to get worried that Jim will find out. So one day he says to Della that it is too risky to keep using the flat. He has a much better idea. From now on they will go out each afternoon on the Hudson River day boat. He has arranged for a cabin in a secluded sector of the upper deck where they can have complete privacy. Unable, as always, to deny him anything, Della agrees.

"They board the boat and he takes her to the upper deck where his cabin is located. The deck, as he promised, is deserted. 'Nice layout, huh?' he says proudly, and he starts for the cabin with her. But at this moment Jim suddenly leaps out from behind a smokestack! 'Aha!' he cries. Jim, it seems, has become suspicious of his wife and on this day he has not gone to work but has trailed her to her rendezvous.

" 'Jim!' cries Della, panic-stricken. 'What are you doing here?'

" 'What,' counters Jim hotly, 'are *you* doing here? And with this loathsome creature?' He points a scornful finger at the little man.

"Della does not wish to cause her husband any pain, so she makes up an innocuous little lie. 'You mean this gentleman here?' she says. 'I was just asking him the time, that's all. Wasn't I, sir?'

"'Yes. Oh yes,' he says with alacrity. He pulls out his watch. 'It is a quarter past two, madam. And now if you'll excuse me——'

"'Oh, no you don't!' thunders Jim. 'Take this, you cad!' And he strikes the little man a blow of such severity that he goes flying over the rail and into the Hudson River below. The deck being deserted, nobody witnesses this occurrence.

"'Help!' shrieks the little man in the water. 'I can't swim.'

"'Save him, Jim,' cries Della wildly. 'You must save him!' Jim, startled by the desperation in her tone, plunges immediately into the river. The little man is sinking. Jim reaches out and grabs his hair. The hair comes off. It is a toupee.

"Now suddenly the reason for the little man's attraction is clear to Della. It is the toupee. *For the toupee is made of her hair!* The little man obviously bought it from the wig-maker to whom she had sold her hair the previous Christmas. Della, as I have pointed out, was terribly proud of her hair. She did not realize it, but after her hair was gone she had a fierce subconscious desire to get it back. When she saw it on the little man, although she did not recognize it consciously, it struck a deep chord in her subconscious. And that was why she was so mysteriously attracted to him: he had her hair.

"But now that Della knows the reason, the spell is

broken. The little man no longer has any hold on her. She looks over the rail and sees Jim churning around in the river, trying mightily to save the little man. 'Never mind, Jim,' she calls. 'Let him drown.'

"Jim forthwith gives up his attempts at rescue and clambers back aboard. She throws herself into his arms, wet as he is. 'Forgive me, Jim,' she begs. 'I've been such a fool.'

" 'It's all right, darling,' he replies tenderly, kissing her contrite tears away. 'It's all right.'

"And then Jim, chancing to look down, sees a watch lying on the deck. The little man dropped it when Jim knocked him overboard. Jim's eyes bulge. *It is Jim's watch!* With a peal of joy he picks it up, puts it in his pocket, and they live happily ever after."

"Holy Jesus Christ," breathed Mr. Young. "Atterbury, this guy is a maniac."

"Read him the last item," said Mr. Atterbury.

The accountant blinked a few times and then picked up his balance sheet. "In the last quarter," he read, "Overmeyer bought merchandise in the amount of $394,024.03, which he borrowed at 2 per cent per annum. Quarterly charge, therefore, is $1794.12." Mr. Young closed his brief case and started for the door.

"When you add the interest charges to the operating expenses," said Mr. Atterbury, rubbing his hands together briskly, "you find that George showed a net loss of $12.44. . . . The store, Harry, is mine."

"Merry Christmas," said Mr. Young.

CHAPTER 21

Business!

I laid a Gladstone bag on my bed and started to pack. (It was a nice bag—real pigskin. The bed was nice, too, though not, of course, pigskin.)

I'd had all of business that I wanted. Duplicity and heartlessness, that was business. Trickery, perfidy, and avarice.

I was through with business, through with Atterbury, through with my loveless marriage, through with Ivanhoe Gardens. I was walking out. I would be poor once more, yes, but never again would I be party to the ruination of another human being in the name of business.

I put a half-dozen shirts into the bag. I took them out again. They were Dad Geddes's shirts, not mine. So, in fact, was the bag. I closed it and stuck it in the closet.

I would go as I had come—in my cheap suit, my un-

Sanforized shirt, my leatherette bow tie. Good-by to luxuriant tweeds and sleek worsteds. Good-by to silk neckties and argyle sox and handmade brogans. Good-by to linen as soft as a caress. Good-by to all that.

Clothes did not make a man. Far better to be shabby and honest; far better to wear rags and eat crusts then to lose one's soul. Crusts, as a matter of fact, were not so bad. They could be mighty tempting when fixed in a bread pudding with raisins. It was not, to be sure, peach Melba, but it was nourishing. (I had grown quite fond of peach Melba. I liked it especially with a hard sauce after sirloin Chateaubriand, or with chopped nuts and grenadine after lobster thermidor.)

But this was no time to be thinking about peach Melba and sirloin Chateaubriand and lobster thermidor. Or about racks of spring lamb or baked squab or chocolate mousse or succulent filet of sole, done to a turn in lemon butter and served with fresh tartar sauce and a sprig of parsley. Good-by to all that. I was going back to pork jowls and decency.

I retched for a moment thinking of pork jowls, but a swig of Courvoisier revived me. (Good-by to that too.)

Back now to poverty and want. Back to my hard life and my pallet, also hard. My soul would be my own once more, and that was worth all the toil and privation I would have to suffer. Wasn't it?

Of course it was.

Was it really?

Certainly. What is a man profited if he shall gain the whole world and lose his own soul?

Yes, that was so. But still——

There was a knock on my bedroom door.

"Come in," I called.

Miss Geddes entered. "Darling!" she exclaimed.

I blinked in astonishment. Perhaps she was confusing me with the gardener; we were the same build.

But no, she was calling me by name now. "Harry darling!" And *kissing* me!

"Miss Geddes," I stammered.

"Call me Esme," she said with a warm smile.

"Oh, how I've wanted to!" I cried. "But what——"

She pinched my cheek. "Aren't you the sly one?" she said playfully. "Well, you don't have to pretend to be a dope any more. Your secret is out."

"My secret?"

"I know all about it now—how you played dumb to win George Overmeyer's confidence, how he trusted you, and how you snatched his business away from him. Brilliant, Harry, brilliant!"

"No, no!" I cried in horror. "It wasn't me."

"Now, you don't have to be modest with me, darling. I know you were working for Atterbury. But it was all your idea. He told me so himself. He told everybody! The whole neighborhood's talking about you, Harry."

I sank to the bed and clutched the bedpost weakly, overwhelmed by the monstrosity of Atterbury's lie. Why, I thought in anguish, was he giving *me* the credit? And then I knew. It was better that way, better for his nefarious purposes. He didn't want people to think him too clever; it might scare away new victims. Oh, infamous, infamous!

"You're the sensation of Ivanhoe Gardens. Everybody's raving about how clever you are. I'll bet thirty people stopped me on the street today to congratulate me . . . What's the matter, Harry? You're white as a ghost."

I shook my head dumbly; speech would not come.

She looked at me with sudden suspicion. "It *was* your idea, wasn't it, Harry?"

All the softness was gone from her now. She stood over me, tense, hard, demanding . . . And lost, lost to me forever unless I lied and said it was my idea to ruin George. Lost, her silken skin; lost, her breasts like young roes, her cunningly hinged thighs, her dimple-kneed, full-calved, slender-ankled legs. Lost, my ripe and fragrant wife, unless I told her it was my idea to ruin my best friend, to steal the bread from his mouth . . . Well, maybe "steal" was too strong a word. It had all been perfectly legal. No law had been broken.

Suddenly I sat up straight. The legality, it occurred to me, was an aspect I had not heretofore considered. *No law had been broken.* Didn't that put rather a new light on everything? After all, George hadn't lost his store at gun point. Nobody had broken and entered; nobody had embezzled or forged or looted or burned. George had been just plain *outsmarted.* It was tough luck, all right, but it was the breaks of the game.

The *game,* yes! That's what business was—a game in which the trophies went to the swift and strong and resourceful, just as in any other game. And just as in any other game, people got hurt. You wouldn't call football or baseball or basketball reprehensible. Then how could you call business reprehensible?

George lost because he wasn't a good player, that's all. It was sad, of course, that he should now be a poor man, without money, without a business. Very sad—— But was it?

For I was suddenly remembering the night I had first seen George at Miss Geddes's house. He had talked that night about two poor boys who got rich. One was smart; one was dumb. The smart one wanted to save the world, but when he had money he got lazy and forgot all about his noble plans. The dumb one was a harmless slob until he got rich. After that he was dangerous.

George had called both these boys hypothetical. But all at once I knew that only the dumb one was hypothetical. The smart one was real. It was George himself!

He had gotten rich and lazy and forgotten his plans to save the world. But I had made him poor again. Now, removed from the stultifying effects of wealth, he would become strong and vital again—a whole man. And he had me to thank for it!

Well, not me, actually. It was really Atterbury's doing. But people believed it was me. That was the important thing: what people believed. After all, what is truth? Truth is what people believe. People believed I outsmarted George; ergo, it was true.

A great weight was lifted from my heart. Business was a game, and I had done George a favor.

Now I would go back to playing the game. Eventually I would become as proficient as any of them. But meanwhile—during my apprenticeship, as it were—I would be mighty careful about having any more dealings with Mr. Atterbury. He had shown himself a formidable player, the old rascal!

Of course I didn't *have* to do business with him any more. With my new reputation as a sharp trader, I would soon have all the clients I wanted. I could tell Mr. Atterbury I was too busy if he came around again . . . Still, if he had some proposition that was *really* interesting——

"Harry," said Miss Geddes sharply, "answer me. It was your idea, wasn't it?"

"Certainly," I said, "Esme."

Her face relaxed into a proud smile. She sat down beside me on the bed and kissed me full on my carmine lips. "That's my darling," she breathed.

"Pshaw," I said, reddening.

She leaned back on the bed and stretched her arms over her head. "I'm so tired, darling," she said languidly. "Isn't it almost bedtime?"

"Yes, it *is* getting late," I said and pulled the shade to keep out the afternoon sun.